WESTCOTT HIGH 3

SARAH MELLO

—

To Michael F

Souls like yours don't stay buried, they fly.

First Printing, 2021

United States of America

ISBN: 978-1-7331743-3-6 (paperback)

Author: Sarah Mello

Editor: Melissa Frey

Book Cover Design: Olivia Heyward

CONTENTS

1 MOMENTS

I once vowed to tell you a story about love, tragedy, and friendship. I promised to write about butterflies and firsts, the bittersweet ups and downs of life's blows, and the hoops we'd jump through to not lose the people most important to us. Some would even say I made good on that promise. But over the pots of coffee and deep into the sleepless nights, I managed to see something through fresh eyes: My story, my *real* story, hadn't yet been told.

Mr. Russell often said that to be a writer, you must look for the defining moments. The pauses in time that shaped you, ruined you, left a mark more permanent than the most regrettable tattoo—there is where you can begin. I remember feeling crushed hearing those words, knowing I was the girl sitting in her room knee-deep in journals and cheesy rom-coms, but he was right. A story isn't a story without them, and until you've experienced those moments, you don't really have one.

But this isn't my goodbye. This isn't where I tell you that everything you've read about me and my friends was inconsequential and reduced to mere memories hidden in the dark recesses of my mind. No. It mattered.

Everything mattered.

The breakups, the makeups, the situations that forced me to accept my purple color wasn't going to set me apart—it all prepared me for that first moment. The first pause in time when I realized my story had just begun.

I had never been inside Westcott High on a Sunday before, but there I was, walking toward the entrance of the school with three tall men in dress clothes leading the way. My mother, wearing a trench coat and blue jeans, walked beside me. The cold air whipped against my face, almost warning me to turn around, and my body was quivering just thinking about what might be coming. I couldn't stop staring at the manila envelope dangling from Principal Winchester's fingers, taunting me. It was so close I could grab it, so tempting I considered it, but I refrained.

"Why didn't you answer your phone when I called?" Mom whispered, her *cà phê sữa đá* breath strong. *Bún chả* might not have been on the dinner menu anymore, but her morning Vietnamese coffee was something she'd never give up.

"Mom," I gritted, keeping my voice low so my words wouldn't travel. "I'll answer your question, but you have to answer one for me first. Where did they get that envelope?"

Principal Winchester, Assistant Principal Clemmons, and Mr. Harrison came to a stop in front of the main office door, and Mom and I did the same as we turned to face each other.

"Under your bed," she replied, staring blankly at me as if I already knew.

"Darcy, if it's all right, I'd like to have a moment to chat with Sonny alone?" Principal Winchester waited for her answer, but it wasn't exactly a question. "When Dirk arrives, the three of us will talk," he added, holding open the door. "Principal Clemmons, if you and Mr. Harrison would lead the way to the conference room, I would appreciate it."

"I don't know," I heard Mom mumble, but not aggressively enough to save me. They led her toward the other side of the office while I followed Principal Winchester to his.

He opened the door and ushered me inside. If he weren't a crooked, lowlife, scumbag of a man, I'd have thanked him.

"Under my bed?" I mouthed to no one, sitting down in a navy-blue guest chair. "How in the—"

"Ms. Carter." Principal Winchester's voice was subdued, like he kind of wanted to talk but really didn't in the slightest. He closed the door and walked behind his desk, and with one hand tucked in the pocket of his slacks, the other reached for a frame. His cheeks drooped as he lifted a photo of a younger

Kyle toward his face. "Do you remember the day you two got stuck in our treehouse?"

I blinked. I had prepared myself for a hot scolding, not a trip down memory lane.

"It was a rickety old thing," he continued. "There when Kate and I bought the house all those years ago. I wanted to tear it down, but she insisted we keep it. She insisted on a lot of silly things, but that's a conversation for another day."

His eyes softened. "You and Kyle loved it. Took board games up there. Coloring books. Little notebooks and binoculars when the two of you spied on the neighbors behind us. Snacks, blankets—hell, we practically had to drag you both out of that thing come nighttime." A grin crept to his lips. "You remember?"

"Y-yeah. I remember."

He paused, and the yellow rays shooting through the blinds melted the smile off his face. "Until the day the ladder fell down. Maybe it wasn't properly secured, maybe the wind blew it over, but there it was, lying on the grass thirteen feet below. I was in my office when I heard you both yelling for me. 'Dad, Mr. Winchester, help us, help us!' Came out back and saw your little heads poking out the window."

He set the picture frame back down and took his seat across from me. "At eight years old, you probably could've jumped and been okay, but you were both terrified. I'm sure you thought your troubles were over when I walked outside.

Probably assumed I was going to put the ladder back up and help you down. But do you remember what I told you, Sonny?"

I glanced south at my lap, trying to recall.

"No?"

"Um." I squinted, desperately searching for the answer he wanted like a soon-to-be first-runner-up in a spelling bee. "No, I, um—"

"I told you to get out." He lifted his head. I lifted mine. The two of us made eye contact for the first time that morning, and something about the way he looked at me summoned tears. "And when you said you couldn't—that there was no way—I told you that there's—"

"—always a way out."

"That's right," he whispered, his grin returning with a vengeance. "There is *always* a way out. You see, I put an escape ladder in that old yellow trunk you and Kyle kept your games in, but you kids didn't know that. You needed someone to come along and tell you that you weren't really stuck. To guide you—to show you—that there was another option. And you eventually found that option, didn't you?"

"Yes." I blinked, and a lonesome tear made its way down my cheek. "We did."

"You did," he repeated. "Sometimes, Ms. Carter, we find ourselves in sticky situations. Stuck in a treehouse with no clear way down or sitting in an office with your principal who received an anonymous tip he'd find a top-secret document underneath your bed."

I went to speak, but he leaned forward and beat me to it.

"I'm not going to ask how you got it, why you have it, or what you planned to do with it—I'm not here for that. But it seems you're in direct violation of the SCC. I hate to say this, Ms. Carter, but you couldn't explain yourself out of this even if you wanted to—tried to—and if I gave you enough rope to do so, you'd likely hang yourself before you started. No one would believe whatever story you've concocted in your head, and without proof, no one would listen to more than ten seconds of it."

I bit the inside of my cheek to stay angry. I knew if I allowed my emotions to take over and started bawling in his office, he'd win. Although, by the looks of it, it seemed as though he already had.

"You're a good friend, Sonny. You've always been there for Kyle, and I know you're trying to help JC, but you don't want to get involved in something that has nothing to do with you. Something you don't fully understand. A situation that could end up ruining your future."

He reached over and plucked a tissue from the box then offered it to me. "You, my friend, have a decision to make. You can sit in the treehouse, wait around to see what happens. You can take your chances and jump. Or you can let me show you how to get out of it."

I stared at the tissue, contemplating whether I should make a deal with the devil.

"Come on, Sonny," he continued, extending his hand further. "Let me help you."

Suddenly, the door flew open and hit the wall behind it. I swiveled in my seat, and a red-faced ex-wrestling coach came barreling through the office. "What the hell do you think you're doing?!"

"Coach Dirk?" Principal Winchester stood, and my mother, Ron, and Principal Clemmons filled the empty spaces in the room.

"No, that was before you fired me, Bob." He grabbed my arm and pulled me to my feet. "You have no right to question my daughter without me present."

Mom stepped forward and pulled me out of the line of fire, which seemed to be about all she could do.

"Dirk, listen—"

"No, you listen to me!" Dad's voice quavered, his face beet red. "I don't want you treating my daughter differently than you would Piper, Kyle, or any other student here, you got that? Unethical. Un—" He caught my gaze, and his words cut off as he clenched his jaw tight. Whatever he saw in my eyes must have calmed him, just a little, because he took a deep breath and stopped talking.

Principal Winchester stalked out from behind his desk and put his hand on my dad's shoulder—a gentle but firm reminder of who really held the power. "Have a seat, Dirk." They made eye contact, and Principal Winchester gave him a quick nod as if to reassure him. "Have a seat."

My parents eventually settled in, and their troublemaker daughter stood behind them, gnawing on her fingernails.

"I didn't want it to be true," he continued, slithering back behind his desk. "But the envelope did contain what we were told it would, and unfortunately, we're going to have to write Sonny up."

"*What*?" I lunged forward. "No! No, you can't!"

"Rules are rules, Ms. Carter."

"But—"

"But what?" Dad whipped around, a scowl darkening his face. "Where the hell did you get that outline? And why do you have it? Huh?!"

"Pull yourself together," Mom mumbled.

"Pull my—" He shot up from his seat, his green wool sweater—the one we bought him for Christmas several years prior—reminding me of simpler times. "I'm trying here, kid. Sure, I've made some mistakes. I haven't always been Father of the Year like every damn coffee mug I own says. But I've been trying my entire life to give you and your sister opportunities. Chances. Second, third, tenth chances—"

"You don't understand . . ."

"Then please explain yourself," Principal Clemmons piled on. "You're going to Yale, Sonny. You have no need for this document." He folded his arms high across his chest. "We need to know why you had it."

"I—"

"More importantly, we need to know who brought it into this school so they can be held accountable."

Maybe I should have told Principal Clemmons that his perfect daughter and colleague conspired together in what could have been considered the greatest ploy in Crescent's history, but I refrained. The last thing I wanted to do was start a war with Winchester—especially one he said I'd never win.

"I, um—" I swallowed. "I don't know what you want me to say . . ."

"How about the truth?" Principal Clemmons quipped.

I scanned the room for an ally, but it didn't take long to realize my only ally in that office was my enemy. And maybe our brief moment of eye contact said what I couldn't, or maybe what happened next was never my call, but before I could blink, Principal Winchester opened the manila envelope, removed the profile, and sealed my fate. "I have an assumption, if no one minds?"

Everyone turned their heads toward him, watching as he peered at the paper, pretending to think. "Been trying to wrap my head around this for hours, and for some reason, Mr. Russell keeps pricking at me."

"Mr. Russell?" Principal Clemmons raised an eyebrow. "How do you figure?"

"Well, he's an alumnus, right? Could have pulled some strings." He glanced up. "And weren't you considering Princeton last year, Sonny? Briefly, I know, but you *were* giving it some thought . . ."

"Mr. Russell was fond of our daughter, Bob, but I don't think he would have funneled that document to her." Mom shook her head. "He could have lost his job over something like that."

"That he could have." Principal Winchester nodded. "But given the way he passed, *something* was eating at him. I hate to think that's what it was . . ."

"Sonny?" Dad poked. "Why don't you tell us? Is this true?"

I was screaming *no* in my head, but nobody could hear me. *Why couldn't they hear me*? Listening to Principal Winchester link me to Mr. Russell's untimely death made my stomach churn—and over a lie, no less. Starting that war was looking more and more appealing, yet I still couldn't ignore the obvious: I wouldn't walk out of it alive.

"Yes," I lied. "It's true."

"What was that?"

"*It's true,*" I replied. "Mr. Russell gave me the profile."

Principal Winchester sighed, almost on cue. "So my suspicions were correct?"

"You know you shouldn't have taken it, right?" Principal Clemmons wasted no time scolding me, and I couldn't help but wonder if he would have been just as tough on Piper. “It wasn’t worth the consequence, Ms. Carter. I’m going to have to write you—”

“Hang on a minute.” Principal Winchester lifted his hand, stopping Clemmons from issuing his judgment. “There might be a way out of all this.”

I steeled myself for his bright idea.

“Dirk, Darcy, as you know, there’s an ongoing investigation into the left-wing fire. The four of us sat in this office not too long ago, discussing rumors that your daughter may have known more about the incident than she was letting on.”

“Didn’t they arrest the Ziegler girl last night?” Dad asked. “What happened with that?”

“It’s complicated,” he answered. “There are many moving parts here, but yes, Ari was taken downtown for questioning.”

“So case closed?”

“Not exactly, Dirk. We’re still missing some pieces to the puzzle, pieces we’re desperate to find. If your daughter is willing to comply, maybe we could work out an exchange to avoid a blemish on her transcript.”

“An exchange?”

Principal Winchester nodded. “If she can give us any helpful information, we can all pretend this meeting never happened.”

“That sounds a whole lot like a bribe,” Dad replied.

"Eh . . . more like an offer." Principal Winchester's grin exposed his wickedness. He sat there smug in his seat while he tested my loyalty like he was certain I had none. "What do you say, Sonny? Will you help us out?"

Maybe he thought I would. Maybe he thought I'd take his shoddy deal because I didn't see another way around it. But I wasn't the same eight-year-old girl who was too paralyzed to find one, so with a false sense of confidence, I mirrored his grin and jumped.

"Like I've said, Principal Winchester—I've told you all I know."

As I laid sprawled across my comforter, I couldn't remember the last time I vegged out on my bed and listened to the sounds my house made. Subtle creaks in the walls as the structure settled kept me guessing, but the clicking sound coming from my door knob pulled me straight out of the game.

I stalked toward the door and jerked it open. Honestly, it was more than what some people would've been brave enough to do.

"*Ky*?"

"Shh!" With his finger over his mouth and his hood over his head, he pushed me back into my room and shut us inside.

"What are you doing here?" I hissed. "I'm grounded!"

"Yeah, no shit." He took his football hoodie off and ran his hand through his dark hair. "Your dad wouldn't let me inside."

"Yet here you are . . ."

"I used the hide-a-key," he explained.

"You wha—"

"I had to dodge him like five times on my way up here." Kyle's chest heaved as he breathed freely—likely for the first time in minutes. "God, your house is huge. Has it always been this huge?"

I shook my head and ripped the key from his fingers. "Seriously, Ky, you can't be here. I'm not allowed to see anyone until the new year, and I'm not exactly interested in extending my sentence."

"Yeah, well, confinement's pretty tough without one of these." He reached into his pocket and pulled out my cell phone. "I took it out of your back pocket at the bakery. Didn't know if your mom was going to search it, and I wasn't sure what she'd find if she did."

"Forgot I even had one," I said, taking it from his hand. "It's over, Ky."

"What's over?"

"Everything."

"'Everything'? What's 'everything'?"

"They found the profile in my room," I groaned, returning to my mattress like it was calling for me.

"The profile? The *Princeton* profile?"

I nodded. "That's why they pulled me from Laurel's this morning. Someone put it under my bed and tipped off your dad. He took me to his office and grilled me before my parents came in, practically demanding I go along with his version of where it came from."

"Which was what?"

I hung my head, unable to keep eye contact for what I said next. "He made everyone believe that Mr. Russell gave me the profile before he died."

"Jesus." Kyle grimaced. "And you went along with that?"

"My only other option was to throw your dad and Piper under the bus, and he made it perfectly clear that would've been the wrong move."

"So my dad has the profile now?"

"He did before he shredded it."

Kyle's face dropped. He dragged my desk chair to the edge of my mattress, took a seat, and begged for more.

"He slipped it into the machine before I left," I continued. "The only sliver of evidence we had against him is sitting at the bottom of his trash can in a hundred pieces."

"Why the *hell* would Piper do this?" he gritted. "Why would she frame you?"

"She didn't," I replied. "It was BC."

"BC? The girl from the bakery?"

"No." I pulled my pillow to my chest, shivering at the thought of her. "The girl who died in a car crash last year."

Kyle deflated, falling back in his seat and folding his arms. "I'm sorry . . . *what*?"

"BC is Jacob's ex from Long Beach," I explained. "She was supposedly killed by a distracted driver. I saw a photo of them in his room, and he told me all about her."

"He told you her name was BC?"

"He told me her name was Claire."

Kyle squinted. "Where have I heard that before?"

"This morning at Laurel's when you met Brystol," I answered.

"Her middle name . . ."

I raised a brow. "We met at the Jefferson homecoming dance, but I didn't recognize her as the girl from the picture. Her hair's a lot shorter now, and it's blonde, but it's her. And she knows I know it. The way she looked at me in the bakery, the way she told me her name, she knows I know *exactly* who she is, and she's trying to ruin my life. She's the one who took the photos of me and Jacob and spread them around school. She's the one who broke into my house and stole my paper!"

"Whoa, whoa, whoa—how do you know all this?"

"Because my flash drive was sticking out of her back pocket this morning." I shot up from my bed and paced, shocked by how quickly I went from vegged out to full-blown panicked. "She must have slipped the profile under my bed before she left."

"I don't understand," he replied, joining me on the carpet. "Why would Jacob tell you she's dead if she's not?"

"Because he's a liar, Ky! He's a liar, and I don't know who he is! None of us do!"

My shouts hung in the air as my words began to sink in. I didn't want them to be true, and part of me still hoped they weren't, but I couldn't ignore the obvious. Jacob Harrison had a story alright, but it wasn't the one he told us.

"So you think BC left you the note? You think she started the fire?"

I pinched the bridge of my nose, preparing myself to tell the second half of the perilous story. "The note wasn't even for me. Mr. Hill left it for Lana."

"*Lana*?"

"That's why she called me this morning," I continued, releasing my grip. "She found it on my nightstand, and based on the way it was folded, she knew it was from him."

"You mean—"

"Yeah." I nodded. "Mr. Hill burned down the left wing."

Kyle stared at my carpet, his mind clearly scrambling to connect the dots. "You're telling me this whole time we thought someone was trying to frame you for arson when—"

"—Hill was trying to frame my sister." I huffed out a quick breath. "What's worse? Our only proof is a piece of paper addressed to no one, signed by no one, and missing a date."

"That isn't proof; that's trash."

"Exactly," I replied. "That's why I didn't even bring it up when your dad offered me a deal."

"A deal? What kind of deal?"

"To give him information on Ari, and in return, he wouldn't write me up for having the profile."

"Did you—"

"Of course not," I replied. "They *want* this to be her. If they find out she was anywhere near the school that night, she's done for."

A glimmer of recognition flickered in his eyes as he realized what that meant.

"It's fine." I shrugged, returning to my bed once again. "It's my first one."

"You only get one," he replied, following me there. Kyle plopped down beside me and stared off into space. "Those assholes seriously wrote you up?"

"With a red pen and everything."

He dropped his face into his hands and sighed. "I'm sorry, Sonny. If I could kill him, I would."

"You know, maybe I'll hold you to that . . ."

"We're going to deal with BC for framing you," he continued. "You know that, right?" I tucked my chin, but he lifted it. "And you know that whatever you decide to do about Jacob, I have your back?"

His words did little to soothe me. After everything that happened back in Principal Winchester's office, I wasn't exactly in the mood to make hard decisions. "I just want to avoid him," I whispered.

Kyle swiped his thumb across my cheek to catch a wayward tear as if he had all the time in the world. "Then we'll avoid him."

"We'll avoid all of it," I replied, my cheeks warming. "Don't tell anyone about BC or the profile or—"

"Hey." He lowered his head to catch my gaze once again. "I won't."

The room fell silent while I sulked, and Kyle gave me time to. He sat beside me without uttering a word but eventually circled back around to more pressing matters. "So what about the rest of it?"

"The rest of what?" I asked.

"The fire, the investigation—"

"You mean the one your evil dad is heading? Ky, I want nothing to do with him, or that, or any of it."

"But—"

"I'm waving the white flag," I interjected.

Kyle stood, and the shouting match resumed. "Sonny, this isn't about my dad! This isn't about the profile, or the setup, or whatever the hell he did to expand. This is about Ari." His eyes softened at the sound of her name. "We have to live with the fact that he's going to get away with what he did to JC. And Piper is going to get away with it. And Guy Penn, and Mrs. Penn, and every other piece of shit who stepped on someone else to get ahead. You're right. It's over. *That* is over. But Ari? The fire? We can't just let them think it was her and move on with our lives!"

"Then what do you suggest we do?" I asked.

His eyes flashed. "We have to get Hill to confess."

"And why would he do that?"

"He wouldn't unless he had to." Kyle glanced at my nightstand. "Do you still have the note?"

"The note? Ky, that note proves nothing."

"*That note* is all we have," he retorted. "We should at least try to use it to our advantage."

I recoiled at the thought. "It's just not a good idea."

"You have any better ones?"

"Well, not at the moment . . ."

"Then it's settled."

"That is not how you negotiate!" I hissed, scooting toward the edge of the bed as he plodded toward the door.

"Meet me at my house tomorrow morning at eight. We'll go pay him a visit."

"Ky—"

"See you tomorrow," he whispered, stepping quietly into the hallway like a sniper. "Bring the note."

Moments. Pauses in time that shape you. The end of a decade, a march down the aisle, the click of the pen used to sign the divorce papers—they all carve you into the person you're destined to become. If you're lucky, you'll experience these moments in the company of loved ones, there to celebrate along with you or to soften the blow.

But if you're anything like me, you'll find yourself standing in the middle of your street with only your neighbor's cat, tightening your bathrobe as you watch the garbage truck disappear into the morning sun . . . and there is nothing lucky about that one.

2 HELP

In Westcott, needing things from others is one of those things you try not to need. You mow your own grass. You pay your own bills. And unless you want them drawing all sorts of conclusions, you never borrow an egg from your neighbor.

Yet, as I've said before, no one can get through life alone. Despite our privilege, not even the elite can get by without a little help. And if I've learned one thing from this treacherous town, it's not so much about the asking—it's about knowing who to ask.

Kyle emerged from his front door the following morning, fresh out of the shower and ready to take on the day. His thick, black hair laid curly atop his head, and his face was still dewy from the steam. I wished I felt half as good as he looked.

"Hey," he mumbled, his eyes narrowing as he stalked toward the driveway. "Are those . . . pajama pants?"

"The note's gone," I blurted out.

"Wait, what?"

"The note—Mr. Hill's note—it's gone."

"What the hell do you mean 'it's gone'?"

"Lana tossed it," I replied, silently scolding myself when I realized too late that I was, in fact, still wearing pajamas. "The garbage trucks had already come by the time I ran outside."

"Shit," Kyle whispered, propping himself up on his SUV with both hands. His head was down, and I feared that was his new normal. "Why would she do that?"

"It's not like she wanted to keep it," I replied. "This is my fault. I should have taken it back from her."

"Little too late for should'ves," he snapped. "What now?"

I glanced up at the sky for answers while simultaneously wondering when it was going to fall on me. "I don't know, Ky. I don't know what to do."

The street fell quiet as we stood there, lost in our thoughts and apparently completely out of ideas. Eventually, Kyle found one.

"You're going to go home and enjoy your Christmas." He pushed himself off his car and turned to face me. "I'll handle it."

"You'll 'handle it'? What does that mean?"

"It means I'll figure it out." His eyes whispered *Don't worry*, but I learned to stop trusting that look after his seventh failed attempt at a healthy relationship with Ari. "Just don't tell anyone about Mr. Hill. Not yet."

"Wait, what? *Why*?"

"Because we can't get him to confess with no leverage," he replied. "I have to find something else, and I don't want to get Ari's hopes up when there could be nothing else to find."

"Confession aside, I think the others would like to know we found the arsonist!"

"Well, until we have his confession—we didn't."

"Ky!" I exhaled. "You can't seriously expect me to keep this from everyone. Let them help us!"

"What for? So we can have ten people stressing instead of two?"

"Maybe we can fill in just a few of them. Maybe Cliff could—"

"I said I'll handle it," he shot back, and I understood his heavy implication that he'd rather choke on eggnog than work alongside his former best friend. "Now promise me you'll keep this information ours."

"Ky—"

"*Promise me, Sonny*."

"Alright!" I caved. "Alright, I promise."

Kyle raised an eyebrow as if regarding my pledge with skepticism, so much so that I started doubting myself. But then he moved on. "Oh, before I forget . . ." He ran back inside, returning with a large bag in hand. "Here's your Christmas gift."

In true Kyle fashion, he used one of the shirts he bought me as tissue paper, but I managed to catch a glimpse of the mountain of clothes underneath it. There were headphones to the left, scrunchies to the right, and a card tucked into the front.

"Here's yours." I reached into my back seat for his new sneakers and pile of gift cards. I didn't come close to being half the gift giver Kyle was—or half the person. "Open it later," I said, trying to avoid that awkward moment when someone out-gifts you.

"Understood." He forced a smile and pulled me in for a hug. "You don't want to hit the gym with me, do you?"

"You know, I would, but I have to get to my mom's so she can have her turn at grounding me."

"Mm-hmm." Kyle lifted his chin off my head. "Love you."

"Yeah," I mumbled, fighting the urge to give up entirely. "Love you, too."

As I watched him drive off into the thick fog that Monday morning, I wasn't scared I was doing the wrong thing by keeping that promise—I was certain I was.

"Christmas sucked harder than a hungry baby," Winston said, starting January off right with a candy cane in one hand and a stash of inappropriate jokes in the other.

"That's . . . new," I replied, scanning the crowd for Jacob as if I'd lost my child in an amusement park. I'd ignored his texts and calls the entire winter break, and I knew he'd come looking for me.

"New Year, new one-liners," Winston replied, strolling by an all-black-wearing brunette to his right. "Big day tomorrow . . ."

Ari passed in my thoughts and so did her school disciplinary proceeding, scheduled bright and early for the following morning. Her arrest was the talk of the town over winter break. Probable cause aside, no one could believe the cops would rip her from our gala in front of the entire student body.

More surprisingly, Westcott's administration didn't seem to be sure they'd be welcoming her back until everything was settled—hence the hearing.

"Huge day," I mumbled, stepping in front of my locker. I turned the dial on the lock then gave it a good shake when the combination didn't work.

"Think they'll let her stay?"

"Not sure," I replied, wrestling on.

"Hey, Sonny?"

"Yes?" I groaned.

"You know this isn't your locker, right?"

I lifted my eyes and saw an unfamiliar number on the plaque. "Right," I answered, shimmying left and hoping to leave that moment behind us.

Thankfully, Winston did. "I can't believe your plan to confront Winchester got derailed at the gala. When are we going to reschedule?"

My body tensed up at the thought. As far as everyone knew, our discovery that Principal Winchester set the fire was as good as gold, and since Kyle forbid me to reveal the true arsonist's identity, all I could do was backpedal.

"Yeah, you know, I'm not so sure we're going to," I replied, opening my actual locker. "After thinking it over, we were probably just grasping at straws."

"*Really*?"

"Yeah." I shook my head, pretending to be disappointed with my work. "It was hard to come to terms with."

"Well, I hope you have something else to grasp at—for Ari's sake, at least." Winston picked at the candy cane stuck to his teeth, accidentally flicking a piece at my face. "You coming tonight?"

"Where to?" I asked, slapping the sticky candy off my cheek.

"Uh, Casey's? Packing party? She's moving into Kyle's this weekend, ring a bell?"

"Shoot." I squeezed my eyes shut. "I forgot all about that."

"For the love of God, don't tell me you're bailing. Thing One and Thing Two are the bane of my existence, and I was counting on you to tackle their room."

"Her *brothers* are adorable."

"They're crazy little monsters," he argued. "One of them stole twenty dollars out of my wallet when Casey and I were baking cookies."

My jaw dropped. "Since when do you bake cookies with other people?"

"Since you decided to get two boyfriends." His eyes lost focus as he stared out into the hallway. "They denied it, but I know I had a crisp Andrew Jackson in there."

"Well, I hope you called in the firing squad."

"Hey!" He came to. "Stealing from the poor is a serious offense! I needed that twenty for gas!"

"They're kids, Winston." I rolled my eyes. "And I do *not* have two boyfriends."

"That's right. I forgot Dean kicked you to the curb."

Dean. The guy I hadn't spoken to since he placed a bouquet of red roses in my hand—roses I let die. He was the reason I couldn't find joy in any Christmas song and the reason I dumped extra M&M's into my holiday trail mix. Truthfully, *he was the reason for everything*.

I hated that we weren't speaking. I hated that he was right about Jacob and that I didn't have the decency to give him the benefit of the doubt. But most of all, I hated that he hurt me—and that I hurt him.

"He didn't kick me to the curb," I replied, my mind traveling back to that night in his driveway.

"Isn't that exactly what he did?"

"Isn't it considered rude to pry?"

Winston shrugged. "Fine. I'd much rather talk about Jacob anyway."

My heart dropped. I hadn't yet caught Winston up to speed, and I still wasn't ready to. "What about him?"

"I saw you two at the gala . . ."

"We were just dancing, Wins."

"Just dancing?" He huffed. "The guy swiped your face at just the right speed."

"Okay, would everyone please stop saying that?!"

"Come on," he nudged. "When are you two going to make it official?"

"I guess when the time is right," I replied, starting toward first. "I'm not sure I'm ready to jump into a new relationship right now."

"Why don't I just push you into it to eliminate doubt?"

"I'd like to push you straight into a—"

"Oh, look, we're here." Winston stopped outside of my classroom and leaned against the doorframe, batting his eyes. "Please try to make it tonight, would ya? The three of us barely hang out anymore."

"Isn't that Casey's fault?" I asked, stepping to the side so a classmate could enter. "She hardly makes time for us now that she's in infatuation with Sawyer."

"She made time for us tonight," he replied.

"She needs help packing, Wins. That's not exactly a selfless offer."

"Neither was your offer to help me clean out my closet last summer."

"Okay, I took like two shirts."

"Three."

"Two and a half. The third one shrunk and had four holes in it."

"Three. That shirt came with holes, and you can easily stretch it back out with my mom's thigh machine."

"Should I even ask?"

"Nope."

"Didn't think so," I replied, drifting into class. My peers were steps ahead of me, already knee-deep in the assignment written across the board. Before my life had taken such a crazy turn, I was that student. I was ahead. I was an overachiever who had her nose in her books long before the bell rang.

I'd fallen hard.

My phone buzzed as soon as my back hit the seat, and I slid my fingers into my pocket to retrieve it. Looking quickly over both shoulders, I tapped the screen and read the text message:

I think we need to talk.
2874 Baker Street
Eleven o'clock.

"What the—"

"Carter!"

I jerked my head up at Cliff and slapped a hand over my heart, smiling at every glowering student to let them know I was okay—not that they cared. "Jesus, Cliff! Do you have to scream my name?"

"If it'll get a response." He stole the chair in front of me and spun around, wasting no time getting to his question. "Why the hell haven't you been answering my calls?"

I hadn't seen Cliff since our ploy to pin Winchester fell to pieces nor had I talked to him since that morning in Laurel's, moments before my world came crashing down. I couldn't put my finger on it, but as he sat before me, a few more hairs on his face than normal, I could tell something was askew. His sling was intact, his khakis were pressed, but still, something was off. I had a terrible feeling it went deeper than skipping a few days of shaving, but I tried to blow past it.

"Lana was home," I answered. "I was spending time with her."

“Couldn’t have slipped away to ping me?”

“That girl loves to bake cookies,” I replied, cursing myself for refusing acting classes when I was nine. “Especially ones in the shape of reindeer. I must’ve decorated two hundred of them . . . every day . . . My fingers were—”

“Cut the shit, Carter.” Cliff’s blue eyes drifted toward black. “Why are you avoiding me, and *don’t* say you were frosting Rudolph.”

“Fine,” I hissed. “I know you want to carry out our plan, but we can’t.”

“And why’s that?”

“Because I don’t think we have the right guy,” I replied.

“The right guy? What the hell do you mean ‘we don’t have the right guy’? We sat in my car for half an hour and pieced it together, Sonny. It’s Winchester. It has to be.”

“I know what we thought, but we were wrong.”

Cliff averted his eyes, cupping his mouth and laughing under his breath. Time was running out on Ari’s clock, and I knew he could sense it. I also knew once I told him about Mr. Hill, he’d feel at ease. But temporarily, of course, since we couldn’t prove it was him.

“Tell me why.”

“Pardon?”

“Tell me why you think we’re wrong,” he mumbled, staring blankly through the classroom window.

My promise to Kyle pricked at me. “I—I can’t.”

“You can’t.”

“No, I can’t, okay? You just have to trust me.”

Cliff nodded, but his silence concerned me. He sat for a moment, just gazing at the glass, then stood to his feet and faced the back of the room. “Yeah, sorry,” he mumbled, leaning over my desk before strolling toward his. “*Can’t.*”

As I pulled into the vacant parking lot of an abandoned warehouse, I could see that 2874 Baker Street wasn’t exactly in my neighborhood. The rusted metal building looked like something out of a horror movie—somewhere you wouldn’t go unless you were being paid to. But I wasn’t an actress, and I certainly wasn’t being compensated for my troubles, so I hadn’t the slightest clue why I wasn’t doing half a donut and speeding toward home.

I drove a little further into the lot, and eventually, my headlights exposed the sender of the text message. I took a slow left turn and parked my car, battling with the idea of leaving for a moment but ultimately giving in.

The noise my handle made as I opened my car door was loud, harsh. I couldn’t recall a time I’d ever noticed its sound, but that night, it sounded like a mistake.

I pushed open the door with my left foot and stepped outside, unable to imagine why I’d do something so irresponsible—go to an empty parking lot alone, so late at night and so far away—but with one last deep breath, I walked around my car and came face-to-face with the homecoming queen.

"Live and in the flesh," said BC, as boastful as ever while standing underneath the lonesome street light. Maybe she'd left her shame at home, or perhaps she wasn't remorseful for being a home intruder who tried ruining my life.

I tucked my hands into my coat pockets, attempting to come across as tough while trying not to cry. "I know who you are."

"Really?" Her voice carried just fine, despite her standing many feet away. "Pieced it all together?"

"Just tell me what you want from me!"

"Oh God." She huffed. "Let's not make this cliché."

"If it's Jacob, you can have him."

She laughed, tugging at her hood and exposing her blonde hair. "I wasn't aware you could give him to me."

"Let's cut the fear mongering," I spat. "Just tell me what you want."

"What do you think?"

"Gee, I don't know, BC. You've been following me around town, standing outside of windows, and breaking into my gala. You tried smearing my reputation with that photo. You planted that profile in my room and tipped off my principal." I slowly shook my head at the thought. "You got me written up, Brystol! Do you have any idea what that means?"

"I know it can't be good."

"Yeah, it wasn't," I replied. "What do you want? I think you want to ruin everything I've worked my entire life to get."

"Nah." BC dragged her tennis shoes across the pavement, sauntering toward me as if time didn't exist. When she was a couple of feet away, she planted her sneakers and gave me a sly leer. "I just wanted a little revenge."

I took a step back. Would it not have been super obvious, I would've taken twenty. "Look, I didn't know Jacob was off limits, okay? I didn't even know you were here with us."

BC's malicious look trailed off, and I could no longer read her.

"I don't know the full backstory," I continued, "but he clearly wrote you off and started over in Westcott. I can understand wanting revenge, BC. I can even understand why you think I deserve the brunt of your anger, but if you could kindly redirect it, that would be awesome. I have enough going on right now."

"It takes two to cuddle, Sonny."

"Technically speaking, that's not exactly true." I lifted my hands and dropped them. "Look, why don't you just leave me out of this? Why don't you just confront Jacob for what he's done to you?"

"Don't worry." BC ran her fingers across the bottom of my hair like a harp, looking up to smile at me as the last strand fell. "I plan to."

Before she could string the other half, I peeled my eyes away from hers and started toward my car. My fumbling fingers struggled to locate my keys, but as soon as they did, I unlocked my door and climbed inside. Without wasting a second, I glanced in my rearview mirror, cranked the engine, and bailed.

Call what happened next an accident, or fate stepping in, or well-deserved. Call it what you wish. Whatever the term, though, it changed my life forever.

"I see you found your phone." His voice was raspy, and I could tell by his tone that he wasn't thrilled to take my call.

"Cliff . . ."

I heard a long pause followed by a yawn and incomprehensible words. "It's one in the morning, Sonny."

"Yeah, I, um—" My eyes bled mascara-tainted tears that burned my cheeks every time the wind blew. "I didn't know who else to call."

"Are you crying?" He exhaled loudly. "Kid, if this is about your boy problems, I really don't give a—"

"I need your help."

If there's one thing I've learned from this treacherous town, it's knowing who to call when you need a little assistance, and more importantly, if not most importantly, *knowing who not to.*

3 UNITY

Some people believe you're only as strong as you are united—and I'd have to agree. When two or more people come together for a cause, unity is important. And when the cause could mean life or death, it's essential.

"What the fuck am I looking at?"

I stared down at the pavement with Cliff, a mere shell of myself, someone I didn't know. My body was shaking and sweating so profusely, I was convinced I'd come down with the flu. Any makeup I was wearing for my first day back at school was halfway down my neck, and my morals? Those were long gone.

"A—" I placed my numb fingers on my bottom lip. "A body?"

"Whose body?"

"Jacob's ex-girlfriend," I whispered, the tone of my voice begging for pity.

Cliff did that thing again—the thing he did with his hand when he heard something slightly comical and completely unbelievable. He cupped his mouth and faked a laugh, then he took a step back and stared around the parking lot.

"It's not what you think," I replied, lunging forward. "I was backing out and—"

"And what?!" he shouted.

"It was an accident."

"An *accident*?"

"Yes, an accident! I didn't mean to hit her. I didn't see her. I—I just—"

Cliff turned, but I grabbed his sleeve before he could leave me there with a corpse. "You have to believe me!"

"Why were you with Jacob's ex in the first place?!"

"BC asked me to meet her here," I answered. "I thought it'd be okay!"

"Who's BC?"

I looked down, and so did he. He looked up, and so did I. His eyes were a little wider that night, a little wetter, and I could tell he really regretted picking up my call.

"Brystol Claire Montgomery," I mumbled. "Jacob called her Claire, and he told me she died in a car wreck." I winced at the irony. "She transferred to Jefferson this year. I met her at the homecoming dance, except she waited until she got her revenge before she told me she was Claire—*the* Claire."

"Revenge? What revenge?"

"She was the one who broke into my room and stole my flash drive."

"That's it?"

"Is that not enough?" I huffed. "I know you don't care about the awards, Cliff, but some of us have sacrificed a lot to be on that list. She stole my paper the night before it was due. I had to—"

"Look, I really don't give a shit about your paper right now."

"She planted the Princeton profile underneath my bed," I blurted out, and Cliff's eyes softened. "She tipped off Principal Winchester."

I finally had his attention, and perhaps a tiny amount of compassion, too.

"He, Clemmons, and Ron Harrison showed up to the bakery with the manila envelope. I ended up sitting in Winchester's office where he convinced my parents that Mr. Russell had given me the profile, then he wrote me up and shredded it."

"I thought Piper had the profile," Cliff questioned, trying to keep up.

"Yeah, so did I."

"Then how did BC get it?"

"Piper must have given it to her," I replied.

"They know each other?"

"Apparently!" I dropped my hands against my thighs. "Principal Winchester said he wouldn't write me up for having it in my possession if I gave him information on Ari and the fire."

"*And*?"

"And I didn't!"

Cliff glanced down but quickly lifted his head when he saw the body beneath him. "Is this why you don't think Winchester set the fire? You think BC did?"

"No." I took a deep breath and tossed my vow to Kyle out the window. "It was Mr. Hill."

"*What*?"

"Lana called me before they showed up to the bakery with the manila envelope. She found the note on my nightstand and recognized the way it was folded."

Cliff clenched his jaw, attempting to act like the news wasn't affecting him, but his face said otherwise.

"Nobody was trying to frame me for arson," I continued. "Mr. Hill was trying to frame Lana."

"You're telling me the note wasn't even for you?!"

"I thought it was!"

"Why the hell haven't you told anyone this?!"

"I—I just—"

"*Why*?" he tried again, only this time, his voice sent shivers down my spine.

"Because Kyle wanted to handle it!"

"Handle it?" Cliff squinted. "How?"

"We were going to try to get Hill to confess by using the note as leverage, but it's gone. Lana threw it out." I folded myself into my jean jacket and shrugged. "Kyle said he was going to find something else."

"And you two didn't think we'd want to know about this?"

"I tried convincing him to tell you guys, but he didn't want the help."

"You mean *my* help."

"Cliff—"

"No, fuck him, okay?! He wasted *weeks* trying to dig up information on Hill instead of coming to us to make a plan." I followed his eyes as they descended, and when I saw that BC's pool of blood had reached my Converse, I burst into tears.

Cliff stepped forward but seemed unwilling to console me. Instead, he shoved me in my shoulder and forced me to straighten. "No. Don't you dare fall apart now."

"We have to call the police," I cried, realizing my bigger problem was bleeding out while I carried on about an old temp.

"And tell them what? You ran over your crush's ex, waited hours, then called me over for a viewing party before you got around to phoning them?" He reached over his head and pulled his hoodie off, his white t-shirt no match for the winter winds. "Think they'll believe this was an accident?"

"It was!"

"It doesn't matter, Sonny! Your credibility is shot."

"Says who?"

"Says your transcript!" He huffed. "You're no better off at this school than your sister was, and while we're on the subject, make sure you tell her I said 'thank you' for boning the teacher who burned down the left wing."

"That wasn't Lana's fault."

"Everything is Lana's fault!" he shouted, pain coating his words. Never had he allowed himself to show such raw emotion over my sister. In fact, I'd never heard him sound that alarmingly honest about anything before.

In that moment, I finally realized what was different about him. Cliff Reynolds, the King of Westcott, was coming undone.

"It's not worth the risk." He held his hoodie out like a grocery bag. "You're going to have to help me help you. Now give me your shoes."

"What—what are you going to do with them?" I asked.

"Burn them."

"What about her?" I untied the laces and dropped my favorite bloodied sneakers into his sweatshirt. "What do we do with her?"

"This warehouse is abandoned and far off the main road. We should be fine until tomorrow."

"And what are we going to do tomorrow?"

"Who knows you know her?" Cliff asked, answering my question with one of his own.

"What?"

"*Who knows you've met her*?"

"Um—" I squinted. I gulped. "JC . . . Kyle . . ."

"Who else?"

"I—I don't—"

"Who else, Sonny? This is important."

"No one!"

"Jacob?"

"No." I shook my head. "No, I never got around to confronting him."

"Good." Cliff wrapped the shoes like a swaddled baby. "And now you can't."

"Wait, what?!"

"Was I not clear?" he spat. "She's going to pop up missing. You didn't know her, and you sure as hell didn't know she was Jacob's ex, do you understand?"

"But—"

"But nothing. As far as Harrison's concerned, you have no idea he lied to you."

"How am I supposed to pretend I don't know?!"

"You're going to figure it out," he replied. "And if I were you, I wouldn't do anything to make him think something's off."

"Why?" I gulped, seriously regretting those declined calls.

"Because when news spreads to Westcott and he realizes she was here, you don't want him to wonder if you pieced it together."

"I don't . . . ?"

"Not unless you want him thinking you had something to do with her disappearance." Cliff lifted a brow. "Better sharpen up those acting skills, Rudolph."

"Where were you last night?"

My head was in my locker, but my mind was still in the parking lot and on the events that took place once I got home. I had stumbled into my bathroom and jumped into the shower, where I scrubbed my skin raw with a soapy loofah. I felt filthy, though I couldn't have been cleaner, and only when the water turned cold did I crawl out onto the bathmat. I put on a robe and reached for my slippers, but suddenly, the idea that some human created a soft shoe to cushion our feet as we walked around our homes seemed asinine.

Before I knew it, the little things I took pleasure in didn't matter one iota, and I was cursing every good thing I crossed paths with. Jail would be my new reality, not fuzzy pink slippers and comfortable bedding. All I could think about was *when* I'd get caught—not if—and it started to eat me alive.

"I'm—" I swallowed. "I'm sorry?"

"Last night? Where were you?"

The noise in the hallway subsided, as if the only two people standing in it were me and the police officer I'd convinced myself was beside me.

"The packing party?" Casey asked. "You didn't show."

I turned my head, finally realizing who it really was. "Oh. Something, um, something came up."

She pushed her glasses up on the brim of her nose, giving me a second to ponder what had just happened.

"Is everything okay?" she asked.

I looked down at her sweatshirt. The name of the college across the front wasn't the one she planned on attending, so I knew it was likely purchased at a thrift store—passed down from person to person until it wound up hanging on a rack. I wanted to hug her; I wanted to feel the touch of her clothing that reminded me of a simpler life, but I refrained.

Maybe I thought she'd find it as weird as I would've. Ever since Sawyer, things just hadn't been the same between us, and she was no longer the friend I ran to amid a crisis.

How Cliff became that person, I hadn't the slightest idea.

"Yeah," I replied, overselling my response. "Just had to change something in my paper."

"Oh, well, priorities." Casey reached into her backpack and pulled out a bag of chocolate chip cookies. "Winston made me aware of your jealousy."

"How sweet of him," I said, taking it from her frail fingers.

"You're coming this weekend, right? To help us move?"

I stared down at the baked goods, deciding to assume I wouldn't be in handcuffs by then. "Yes," I muttered. "I'll be there."

Just then, a large hand wrapped around my shoulder, and the familiar smell of cedarwood surrounded me. My heart sunk to the tile as I turned around, steeling myself for a long-overdue conversation.

"Can we talk?" Jacob asked, letting his fingers slide down my arm.

I felt I was staring at a stranger for more than one reason. Over break, he'd let his facial hair grow into a small beard, his messy brown hair was a little longer, and black bags cupped his eyes. Familiarizing him was the dark-green, long-sleeved shirt he'd picked that morning. It accentuated his biceps, agreeing with him like everything else he'd ever worn.

"Yeah," I mumbled. "Yeah, sure."

Casey pressed her lips together and walked backward into the crowd. When she was out of earshot, he asked me the burning question I knew was coming.

"Is everything okay?"

I wanted to tell him the truth, but when I saw Cliff standing down the hall staring me down like prey, I knew I had to keep my mouth shut. "Everything's fine; why?"

He studied me. "I just feel like something's off between us. You've been kind of distant."

"Oh, yeah, well, Lana's been home. I've been super busy with family stuff."

"Family stuff?"

"She gets super clingy around the holidays," I continued. "Barely lets me look at my phone."

He squinted. "You sure I didn't do something to upset you? You can tell me if I did."

"Yeah, no." I bit my tongue so hard it nearly fell off. "We're all good."

Jacob peered at me like he didn't quite believe that. "Well, I'm glad," he mumbled. "Not talking to you was the worst."

"I'm sure worse things have happened . . ."

While he gently tucked my hair behind my ear, his eyes made up for lost time, soaking in every minute he'd missed over break. "Not to me."

My cheeks began to burn as his fingers grazed my neck, and I quickly had to remind myself of who he really was—or, rather, that I didn't know who.

He probably anticipated spending more time with me, not less, after expressing his love through a note left behind on my pillow. After our dance at the gala, I'm sure he thought we were on the fast track to a relationship. And maybe we were. And maybe it would have been great. Maybe I *did* picture myself with someone other than Dean. With someone like Jacob. *With Jacob.*

But all of that was over, and all that remained was the task of pretending that it wasn't.

"I have to get to first," he said, lifting a brow mid-turn. "I'll text you."

As soon as he was out of sight, I marched down the hall toward Cliff, who turned his head the second he saw me coming. "We have to do something," I demanded, coming to an abrupt stop beside his locker. "I didn't sleep, I can't eat, and I'm—I'm—I'm starting to see things."

Cliff slammed his locker to shut me up. His bony fingers rested upon the cold metal, and his eyes instinctively closed. "She lost."

"Lost? Who lost? What are you—"

"Ari," he replied, cutting his eyes at me. "She lost her case."

"*They expelled her*?!"

"Until."

I let out a deep breath, forcing a smile at Kyle as he strolled by with a fellow brock. I could tell he wanted to know why I was speaking to Cliff so early in the morning—or, rather, at all—but he walked on.

"She can do schooling online, but she can't be on campus." Cliff readjusted his sling like he was three seconds away from chucking it down the hall. His desperation to help Ari was more obvious than the injury he was hiding from his coach, but he'd never admit to either. "Her dad hired an attorney to represent her in the investigation."

"You can't be serious," I said. "*An attorney*? That's where this is heading?"

"It's already there," he replied. "She stopped talking, which means they'll try even harder to get us to."

"Well, they can try, but we won't."

"You're right." Cliff nodded, giving me an uncomfortably long once-over. "Because we're going to make sure of it."

"Is that Terracotta 672?" Winston asked, staring down at BC's pale cheek. "My mom wears that exact shade."

We stood in the parking lot, the ten of us, hovering over her dead body in a perfect circle. By day two, she almost felt more like a burden than a tragedy, and the need to get rid of her was nipping at my ankles.

"No . . ." Norah stepped forward and kneeled beside BC as if she were a detective on the scene. I hadn't seen her since the gala, where she essentially told me I owed her my life, and ironically enough, I soon would. "If my eyes aren't failing me, I think that's Terracotta 679."

Dean yanked her up. "What the hell is going on?!"

I glanced his way, but I couldn't say I liked what I saw. He was wearing his freshman basketball hoodie—the one he used to wear before his life fell apart. It had been through the washer so many times that the fabric was thin and faded, yet I knew it was more dependable for him than any other.

His joggers were wrinkled, which told me he'd been living in them for days, and his skin looked dull, which confirmed my fear that he hadn't been sleeping well since our conversation at the gala.

Dean was bad at loving himself. To him, the only person worth loving was me. When he realized the way in which he loved me was going to have to change, it flipped his world upside down—hence his appearance.

"There's been an accident," Cliff addressed the group, and thank God he did, because I couldn't gather my thoughts after seeing Dean.

"An accident?" Buckets pulled his hunter-green beanie down over his ears, and I had never seen him look so confused. Normally, he had things figured out before the rest of us, but that night defied what we knew as normal.

"Who is this?" Casey asked, burying herself into her sweatshirt.

"BC . . ."

All at once, everyone turned their attention toward the Princess of Westcott.

"You knew her?" JC asked Piper, staring at his former classmate on the concrete below.

She tucked her shiny locks behind her ears, exposing her pearl earrings. They looked new, likely a Christmas present, and I had no idea why it mattered. "I've just seen her around . . ."

"Cut the shit, Clemmons." Cliff chimed in. "How did she know about the profile?"

"I—I think it came up in conversation," Piper replied.

"How did she get it?"

"Well, I gave it to her."

"Why?"

When she hesitated, clearly searching for an answer better than the truth, Cliff tried again. "*Why*?!"

"She was giving me pills," Piper shouted, berry-red circles on her cheeks. Suddenly, the orange bottles Kyle and I found in her nightstand the night of the fall dance made sense.

"*Pills*?"

"To help me focus," she explained, but a Westcott student admitting to taking drugs for cognitive enhancement was almost as embarrassing as getting caught cheating on a test, so her cheeks turned darker, heading toward sangria. "When she asked for the profile, I just felt like I owed her." Her eyes slowly narrowed. "Wait, why are you asking me this? How do *you* know I told her about it? How do you know she had it?"

For the following ten minutes, I caught everyone up on the recent events, leaving no stone unturned while periodically glancing at Kyle in apology.

"I had no idea BC was going to use it to frame you!" Piper pleaded her case. "I—I thought she was asking for it because she was trying to get into Princeton, and I swear I had no clue she was Jacob's ex!"

"It's gone?" JC mumbled. "He shredded it?"

I nodded, pained to see reality hit him. "Principal Winchester offered me a deal to tell them what I knew about Ari and the fire, and in exchange, he wouldn't write me up."

"Well, did you tell him it was Hill?"

"I didn't think it'd matter," I replied. "Our proof that wasn't really proof to begin with is sitting at the bottom of the dump."

"Okay? Then did you tell him Ari was in the woods that night?"

"No," Cliff quickly answered for me. "And neither will any of you."

His sentence silenced the parking lot, and only the crackling of the wind assured me I hadn't fallen into some dark abyss. The time had come to let them know the real reason we brought them there, and nothing could have prepared me for it. That moment—that pause in time when I stared into my friends' eyes and realized they'd never look at me the same way again—was where my real story began.

"We're moving this body," he mumbled. "All of us."

Innocent, confused eyes cut left to right, searching for someone, anyone, to give them clarity. I hated watching my friends drown in front of me before they even knew they'd walked into water.

Norah was the first one to reach for a buoy, and though I expected her to come back with some spitfire response, the only thing she seemed to be able to mutter was—

"*Why*?"

"Incentive." Cliff glanced down at the grim scene beneath him. "There's no reason for any of you to keep your mouths shut about that night. I'm not even sure one of us standing here hasn't already talked. A few days after we were questioned individually, Ari was taken downtown."

"That doesn't mean anything," Norah argued, grabbing the fabric over her heart with coral paint-stained fingers. "The admin found her phone. They've suspected her this entire time."

"And they still do," he replied. "Even more so today than they did a month ago, and do you know what that means, Norah? That means they'll start putting pressure on us until somebody cracks and gives them their smoking gun."

"There is no smoking gun," she retorted. "Ari didn't do it!"

"Which is exactly why we have to do this," he replied. "Ari's dad hired an attorney, and on the off chance he clears her name, it's only a matter of time before they narrow in on their next target."

"One of us?"

"You were interrogated like I was, weren't you?" Cliff pulled his eyes off Norah and scanned the circle. "Someone standing here will be next; there's no doubt in my mind. We move this body together, and we all have the assurance that none of us will talk."

"I wasn't even in the woods that night," Casey cried, tears I tried to ignore streaming down her cheeks. "I wasn't even there!"

"Yeah, but you know we were." He turned to glare at Piper. "And now, so do you."

"I had nothing to do with this!" Piper yelled. "Why would you bring me here?"

"Because we've all seen what you're willing to do if given the opportunity. Had you found out we were near the school that night—"

"I wouldn't have said a word!"

Cliff shrugged. "Didn't really want to chance it, Clemmons."

Kyle dragged his feet across the circle, and all at once, everyone turned their attention toward him. His face was hidden beneath the shadow of his gray hood, and his eyes were dead. Whatever spark that made us humans human was gone, and just a shell of himself was left.

He planted his feet, and with only BC's body between them, he lifted his chin and peered into Cliff's eyes.

With an inch or two advantage over his running back, Cliff glowered down on him. I wasn't sure what they were communicating in their stare, but I knew it was nothing good.

"I know you didn't come here expecting us to agree," Kyle said. "So what happens when we say no?"

"You don't want to do that."

"I want to know why I don't," he replied.

Cliff didn't speak, but when I looked closely, I could read his response in the dark corners of his irises.

Kyle slowly nodded, resigned understanding hunching his shoulders. "You have a story ready to go?"

"One that would pin this entire accident on you." Cliff glanced down at the lifeless pile of leverage between them. "Like I said, you don't want to do that."

"This is bullshit!" Buckets exclaimed. "I'll tell the police you're framing me."

"Why would I do something like that?" Cliff peeled his eyes off Kyle and trained them on Buckets. "Frame you for a random murder? I don't even know you."

"I'll prove it."

"Guess it'll be my prominent attorney's word versus whatever court-appointed one you're awarded," Cliff replied. "You really want to risk it, Cobalt?"

"Not all of us are Cobalts," JC argued.

"Yeah." He nodded. "And not all of us are Cliff Reynolds."

JC clenched his jaw but seemed unable to respond—or, rather, argue. "How did this even happen? How did BC get here when just yesterday she was sitting behind me in calculus?"

Cliff cut his eyes at me, and JC's followed. He stared at me—through me—and his eyes flashed with understanding before I had time to come up with an explanation. "Oh, holy shit," he whispered. "You did this."

"I—"

"You killed her."

"I—I didn't mean to," I stammered. "We were just talking . . . I was just leaving . . . I didn't see her standing there."

"You're blackmailing us," Norah whispered, a statement as much as it was a question. She folded her arms and waited for me to disagree. "*You're* blackmailing us?!"

"They both are," Piper piled on.

"Look, I wouldn't word it that way! We're just using this bad situation to help Ari! To help us! It's security!"

"What an interesting way of saying *yes*," Norah gritted.

"Come on, guys, don't you get it? Don't any of you see the benefit in this?"

Nobody nodded, but they didn't exactly say no either. It was almost as if they hated how illegal the good idea was.

"Why didn't you just handle this yourself?" Piper asked.

"How?"

"By turning yourself in," she shouted. "You should have called the police!"

There it was . . . *the ugly truth.*

That's exactly what normal people would have done. Normal people don't hide dead bodies in lieu of sounding the alarm—they wouldn't even think to.

She was right; I should have. And maybe knowing that I didn't terrified me more than anything. Maybe the grim discovery that I wasn't so normal would be the new bane of my existence. But by then, I'd already believed that turning myself in wasn't worth the risk, and there was no way I was going to.

I stared into the eyes of my riddle-chasing, cookie-baking, strawberry-milkshake-drinking lifers, hoping one of them would realize that so I didn't have to say it. Not surprisingly, Kyle did.

"Where do we put her?" he mumbled, refusing to look at me. I couldn't blame him. I couldn't look at me either.

"The woods," Cliff replied. We all followed him as he turned his head to the left of the abandoned warehouse where a sheet of tall oaks would soon hold our darkest secret yet. "Grab something," he demanded. "*Everyone.*"

Some people believe you're only as strong as you are united. Then again, when you and your friends are carrying a two-day-old corpse to a shallow grave in the middle of the woods, I'm not so sure you're either.

4 WEAKNESS

Weakness: The state or condition of lacking strength. By definition, being weak sounds inevitable. The human soul is rational but flawed, and it will often compromise our ability to see the light at the end of the tunnel. Sometimes, being strong just isn't an option . . . sometimes, you don't want it to be.

I stumbled out of the woods, no knowledge of who or what was beside me. I made it to my car, but I had no sense of depth or time.

I could still feel BC's cold wrist in my hand. I could still see her dangling head as we walked her to her final resting spot. The thud of her body hitting the packed dirt followed me into the front seat, and I wailed uncontrollably in hopes of drowning it out.

Burying her, covering this up sounded better in theory, as these things always do. But I never expected to feel such remorse. BC had done terrible things to me, yet I mourned her. She was shameless in her pursuit to take me down, and yet I was the one feeling shame that refused to stay in the woods with her body. That shame was now part of me—in me—and there was no escaping the ruthlessness of my crime.

"Dean!" I dragged my eyes off the windshield and stepped outside, stopping him before he could reach his car. His head hung low as he flicked his fingers up and down repeatedly, likely attempting to rid them of the feel of her touch. "Dean, wait!"

He slowly turned around, and we stood face-to-face. Naively, I thought he'd have something to say. I thought there was a slight chance he understood why I forced their hands, that it was in everyone's best interest, but he just wasn't there yet.

"*What happened to you*?"

His words cut my attempt at a connection off at the knee. I pulled my head back and let out a quick breath, gazing at him with wide eyes. "Dean . . ."

"Seventeen months," he interjected, jerking his car door open. "I have to share this town with you for seventeen more months . . . and then I never want to see you again."

"See it?"

There, in the middle of a vacant field, sat a rusty, abandoned trampoline. I should have been more interested, but driving home to find Jacob sitting on my front porch with an activity planned was the last thing I had in mind for the evening. All I wanted to do was shower and shower again. I wanted to be left alone so I could get used to it and cry myself to sleep over Dean's powerful words. Jumping on a dingy tarp was nowhere on my list.

"The trampoline?"

"Ah, see, not just any trampoline." He started toward the contraption with a particularly exhausting eagerness. "This is the *truth trampoline*."

I followed, trying to keep eyes on the small beacon of light coming from his flashlight. "I, um, I don't know what that is."

"You will," Jacob replied with a laugh. I found it hard to believe he could smile and carry on like nothing was wrong and not once realize that everything was.

"I heard some seniors talking about it," he continued. "Apparently, the family who used to live here left it when they moved."

"Someone lived here?" My eyes darted from left to right, unable to see much, but I knew for a fact there wasn't a home nearby.

"House fire," he replied, placing his palms on the cold metal frame. "Now it's just a place for teenagers to play drinking games on Friday nights."

"And what about on Tuesday nights?"

Jacob turned around and held out his hand. "Let me help you on."

"I don't—I—"

"Come on." He grabbed my fingers and pulled me toward him. "It'll be fun."

I stared down at our grip, wondering what he'd say if only he knew where my hand had been. "I'm, um—" I pulled it away. "I'm tired, Jacob."

"So lie down with me," he replied, hopping on the trampoline. "We'll play a game."

"A game?"

"*To Tell You the Truth.*"

His words hit my ears like an infection—oh, the irony. What did Jacob know about the truth?

"Come on," he tried again. "I'll explain it once you're up here."

I reluctantly climbed on. The mat felt wet, and I shuddered to think what critters were crawling around me as I laid down beside him.

"You cold?"

I was freezing. "No, I'm okay."

"You sure? I can give you my hoodie."

"Positive," I lied, trying to control my chattering teeth. "So what's this game?"

He turned back toward the sky. "To tell you the truth . . . I drove by your house three times over winter break."

"*What*?"

"That's the game," he replied, nudging me in the side. "You respond to what I said—truthfully—and we both keep going until one of us can't be honest anymore."

"What happens then?"

"Well." He paused. "I guess the loser has to partake in some form of cruel and unusual punishment."

"Sounds a little extreme . . ."

"Better be honest, then." His breath hit the side of my neck, and I could feel his eyes on me. "To tell you the truth, it was five times."

With so many *truths* flying around, I was surprised he couldn't see the one slapping him across the face. I didn't want to be there enjoying his company and stupid jokes. I didn't want to be playing that silly game.

His naiveness was my gain.

"To tell you the truth, I, um—" I shook my head. "I wasn't exactly busy with family stuff?"

"That's a good one!"

"It is?"

"I mean, not for me." Jacob's breath returned. "But I figured that was the case."

"You did . . . ?"

“Yeah,” he replied. “I, uh, I thought you were mad at me for fighting with Dean at the gala.”

“That was two truths,” I mumbled, brushing past that topic before our conversation from the parking lot crushed me all over again.

He rolled on his side to face me. “I see you can count.”

“At least to two,” I replied, searching for my next response. “To tell you the truth . . . I’ve just had a lot going on.”

“I see.” Jacob gulped. “To tell you the truth, not speaking to you did weird things to me. Things I didn’t like.”

“Hence the drive-bys,” I mumbled.

“Hence the drive-bys,” he repeated, letting out a small laugh. “Nah, it was, uh—” I instinctively turned my head toward his, and I could almost feel his lips. The smell of mint lingered between us, and the rush of not knowing how far away our faces were in the inky blackness had my heart doing somersaults. “It was lonely.”

I looked away, but Jacob cupped the side of my face and turned it back. His thumb resting by my ear, he moved his fingers up and down on my neck, and every inch of my body was trembling.

“I, um . . . I don’t think this is how you play the game.”

“No?”

“No,” I managed to whisper seconds before Jacob’s lips crashed softly into mine. He took his time pulling away but quickly returned.

I toppled over, and he followed, pressing into our kiss as he hovered over me. So many things were running through my mind, so many words, but I couldn't speak.

His warm hand crept underneath my shirt, and almost immediately BC's cold body came to mind. I placed my fingers on top of his. It was only a matter of time before Jacob realized I was sobbing, and not surprisingly, he didn't take long to notice.

"What's wrong?" he asked, pulling his head back.

I slapped my hand over my mouth and squeezed my eyes shut. I knew he couldn't see me, and I found some comfort in knowing I could ugly-cry and get away with it.

"Sonny, what's wrong?" he tried again.

I attempted to dig deep but managed to lose the game, and more sobs broke free. "Nothing."

"Did I—did I hurt you?"

"No."

"I'm sorry, I just, I thought—"

I sat up, moving him off me along the way. I knew that wasn't what Cliff meant when he told me to pretend like everything was okay between us, but the night's gruesome misdeed had wreaked havoc on my body, and I couldn't put it aside—not even to act.

"Hey." He grabbed my face, rubbing his thumbs across my tears. "We can stop."

"I'm sorry . . ."

"No, I'm sorry," he replied. "I told you I would wait, and I shouldn't have pushed you."

"Wait? Wait for what?"

"Until you were ready." The words Jacob so sweetly vowed while we danced amongst the Christmas trees flashed across my mind. And there it was: *my excuse*.

Maybe I should have felt guilty for allowing him to think my tears were caused by not being over Dean. Maybe I shouldn't have milked that—used that as my reason for being standoffish. At the very least, maybe I should have felt shame for using Dean's sweet name in my twisted charade. But if it was going to keep Jacob's lying lips off me, I didn't think he would have cared.

"Come on," Jacob mumbled, grabbing my hand. "I'll drive you home."

Sometimes being weak is inevitable. Other times, when the alternative is jumping into a relationship with an incredibly handsome defrauder, it's a choice.

5 SILENCE

Have you ever wondered why we vow to be silent to commemorate important events? Why we undergo a period of noiseless contemplation, prayer, or thought as if it proves we care?

I always found it odd that removing hats and bowing heads is supposed to be a gesture of homage, when realistically speaking, being silent is the laziest form of emotion we humans express. It's just a pause, really. A brief and quiet pause we take to show respect.

Unless, of course, you're pausing to observe your world flipping upside down. Those are loud as—

"Sheets?"

"Figured you could use some new ones," I replied, staring through Casey's lavender frames. "And these have cute little palm trees on them. Look."

"Super cute," Casey replied, shoving the set back into the overpriced gift bag. "I'm pretty sure Ms. Winchester already purchased some."

"Of course." I nodded, swallowing my disappointment. "But hey, you can't have too many spares, am I right?"

Casey glanced at me but quickly looked away. This was the first time I'd seen her since that terrible evening, and the morning of her big move was off to an incredibly awkward start. I knew she was trying her best to see past my shortcomings, but I wasn't too naive to realize our friendship as I knew it was over.

"I should, um—" She stood up from her bed and grabbed a large box stuffed with shoes. "I should keep packing. The others will be here soon."

"Right," I replied, picking up the wads of tissue paper. "I'll just go . . . throw this away."

Without giving her a chance to kick me again, I saw myself out, making my way down her narrow hallway with my tail tucked. The mauve carpet felt sticky between my toes, and for a moment, I wondered if it had ever been vacuumed.

I was relieved when Kyle's offer to Casey worked out smoother than silk but surprised at how fast things were moving. Based on the half-inch layer of gunk on my feet, that move was probably for the best.

"Well, if it isn't Bonnie."

I turned my head toward the kitchen as I trotted down the steps, glancing at Winston while he emptied his bag of packing tape. His hair was untamed, and his face looked unwashed.

In the days following that night, no one had been their normal selves. We agreed to leave what we'd done underneath the oaks, but after seeing Piper Clemmons walk the halls wearing a hoodie and sweatpants, I wasn't so sure our transgression hadn't followed some of us home.

Once I saw Winston's scruffy demeanor, I was certain it had.

"If that means Cliff is my Clyde, then I strongly disavow." I planted my feet in front of him as our friendship hung in the balance—a friendship I didn't deserve. Winston was an innocent soul who liked baking and eating and eating what he baked with friends while watching twenty-year-old rom-coms. He was too good for the evil I'd dragged him into. He was too good for me, too. "You don't have to use humor on this one. You know that, right?"

"It's what I do," he eventually replied, putting my uncertainty to rest. "I make borderline inappropriate jokes, and you follow them up with sometimes funnier, witty one-liners."

"Often funnier," I whispered, letting out a deep breath.

He slowly shook his head, and tears I'd never seen him cry filled his eyes. "You've really done it this time, Sonny."

"Yeah . . . I know."

Winston cleared his throat and turned the page. "Carrying around tissue paper so it looks like you're helping?"

"Oh, good," I replied, attempting the same. "I was hoping it was working."

He pulled the last roll of tape out of his bag and laid it on the cluttered countertop. "Have you talked to her yet?"

"Briefly." I tossed the wad into the trash can and dropped down onto a barstool. "And she hates me as much as I thought she did."

"Casey doesn't hate anyone."

"She can't even look at me," I replied.

"You're not that easy to look at."

I tilted my head, considered chucking a banana from the bunch in front of me at his, but I refrained.

"Look, just give her some space. Everything will be normal again soon."

"Were things normal to begin with?" I asked. "Be honest, Winston. She hasn't treated me the same since she and Sawyer started doing whatever it is they're doing."

"Well, you do loathe the guy she likes," he replied. "I can see how that would create some tension."

"She shouldn't like him."

"But she does."

"But she shouldn't," I argued. "If she even knew half the stuff I know about him, she'd . . ." My words petered out as I followed Winston's gaze toward the right of the room where Kyle stood waiting.

Our eyes met, and the conversation I'd been avoiding for days had finally found me. "Wins, can you give us some—"

"Yep." He scooped the tape into his arms and stumbled backward toward the staircase, dropping a roll beside Kyle's feet along the way. "Pardon, if I could just—" He kneeled. "Oh, are those new kicks?"

Kyle's death glare never left me despite Winston's attempt to lighten the mood.

"I'll give you two some privacy," he said, glancing back at me in apology before treading up the stairs. When he was finally gone, Kyle stalked into the kitchen and leaned against the counter, seeming to want to soak in the silence while he could.

"Why didn't you call me that night?" he eventually asked.

My eyes glossed over at the sound of his voice, and I let out the breath I'd been holding for well over a minute. "I can't answer that."

"Try."

A tear fled from my eye as I searched for the right words, and I realized fairly quickly that there weren't any. "I just didn't, Ky. I wish I had a better answer, but I don't."

He nodded. "You find yourself in a crisis, and it never crosses your mind to call your best friend?"

"Why does that matter?"

"It *matters* because I would have told you to go to the police."

"To be fair, I didn't know Cliff was going to suggest we cover it up."

"Jesus." Kyle pushed himself off the counter, and our conversation picked up speed. "What noble thing did you think Cliff Reynolds was going to suggest you do? It's *Cliff*, Sonny. He charges his mom twenty bucks when she uses his car."

"Okay, so he's slightly obsessed with money . . ."

"He has no morals," Kyle shot back.

I folded my arms, slowly shaking my head while I glanced around the kitchen.

"Oh, you disagree?"

"I didn't say that . . ."

"No, no, go ahead. Please tell me why you suddenly think the person who hooked up with my girlfriend is such a stand-up guy."

"*He helped me*," I fired back. "He could have left me there or turned me in, but he helped me see the truth."

"Which is what?"

"That going to the police wasn't worth the risk!" I looked him up and down as if he should have known. "What if they hadn't believed me, Ky? Then what?"

"Look, I don't have all the answers."

"Which is exactly why I didn't call you!"

Kyle's face dropped, and mine wasn't too far behind his. "I—I didn't mean it like that . . ."

"No, I think you did."

"Ky—"

"Stop saying that!"

"What do you want me to say?!"

He shook his head.

"Look, I realize co-signing Cliff's plan was shocking to all of you, but at the end of the day, he's right. If Ari's attorney manages to clear her name, one of us will be next. The stakes will be higher then. You really want to place your bet on Norah Soros having your back? Trust she won't come up with some crazy story that pins the fire on you?" I softened my voice. "I didn't do this because I'm some monster, Ky. I did this to ensure Ari was safe—and that the rest of us would be, too."

"You have a way with words, Sonny, but you can't rewrite this one. *You blackmailed your friends into committing a crime.*"

"I did what I had to do," I replied. "Cliff helped me, I helped him, and in return, everyone walked away a heck of a lot safer than when we walked into that parking lot."

"Safer?" Kyle huffed. "What happens if someone finds BC?"

"They won't."

"Our prints are all over her!"

"They won't," I replied. "Cliff assured me. If we even thought that was a possibility, we never would have suggested it."

"'We,'" Kyle repeated, squinting his eyes. "You know what? Since when did you become so close with Cliff?"

"We're not close!"

"You're supposed to be my best friend."

"I am!"

"Then stop speaking to him!" he shouted. "No more side conversations. No more conspiring. No more friendship."

"There *is* no friendship, Ky!"

"Good . . . because that would mean the end of ours." Kyle's threat punched me in the gut. He'd never even come close to insinuating our relationship could be in question—much less over something as trivial as me talking to Cliff.

But perhaps losing Ari to his former right-hand man was enough. Perhaps the thought of losing me, too, was unimaginable—hence the bulging veins and bruised ego.

"Do I have your word?"

"Address?"

I slipped Cliff the sticky note before I climbed into the passenger seat of his Mercedes, glancing over my shoulder for Kyle even though I knew he wasn't there. Had he known I was scheming with Cliff less than twenty-four hours after vowing to never speak to him again, our fallout would have been extra brutal.

I felt guilty for making a promise I didn't intend to keep. The truth was, nothing meant more to me than staying two steps ahead of the BC situation. While everyone else wanted to forget about it, I felt a sense of responsibility to babysit it. Apparently, so did Cliff.

"Seat belt," he said, typing Brystol's address into his GPS.

I buckled but never did settle in. The morning was moving fast, our conversation faster. "You sure about this?"

"I'm sure," he replied, turning on my seat warmer. "Just a quick drive-by to see if anything looks off."

I watched his finger leave the button. "I'm still surprised we haven't heard anything yet. It's been days."

"That I can't explain." Cliff pulled off down his street. "She should have been reported missing by now."

"And when she is?"

"We keep our heads," he answered, not knowing some of us were already failing to.

"Any news on Ari?" I asked, pushing Kyle to the back of my mind.

"Saw her yesterday," he replied. "We didn't talk about her case much."

"Overwhelmed?"

"Depressed." Cliff pulled up to a yellow light. "She can't fall asleep at her house, so she slept the day away at mine."

"You must make her feel safe."

"Sure," he replied, shrugging like it was nothing.

My eyes instinctively rolled as I faced forward. "Why do you do that?"

"Do what?"

"Take every sweet moment and stomp on it until there's nothing left."

Cliff glanced at the side of my face. "I didn't realize it bothered you so much."

"What bothers me is you pretending your feelings for Ari are insignificant; you so clearly love the girl."

"Strong word."

"Right word?"

He huffed. "Loving someone doesn't automatically make things significant."

"So what would?"

"Commitment," he replied. "And that's something I can't give her."

"Why not?"

"Because."

"Because *why*?"

"Because it's crossing a line." Cliff lifted a brow to shut me up. "I'm not going to date Kyle's ex."

"But you'll hook up with her?"

"That's different."

"It's worse," I retorted. "Look, Kyle and Ari are done, and there's zero chance he could hate you any more than he already does, so what does it matter?"

"It matters." Cliff shifted in his seat. "And why are you campaigning for our relationship? Since when do you care if we're together?"

"I don't."

"Good," he replied, reaching down to drown me out with music. "Let's keep it that way."

"Cliff?"

He turned the volume up louder, glaring through the windshield as if I'd overstepped—jaw clenched and everything. I don't think he realized his reaction only confirmed he wanted that relationship, but I didn't poke the bear.

Mansions turned to modest two-story houses the closer we got to our destination, and eventually, the GPS directed Cliff to take a left into BC's neighborhood.

"We're here," I mumbled, sitting up straight.

Cliff's eyes darted around, and I could tell his fight-or-flight instincts had kicked in. "Put your hood on," he said before pushing the visors down and turning off his playlist.

My heart began to race as we passed by every California bungalow. There was no shortage of white stucco on the street, and the sloped roofs brought a certain charm to the neighborhood. But the dead grass in nearly every yard was a faded shade of yellow, the mailboxes were all boring black with white letters, and the cars, for the most part, seemed to be older makes.

"Six hundred feet," he mumbled.

"Slow down so we don't miss it!"

And he did, almost too much.

Cliff leaned forward and peered into his side-view mirror. "Shit," he whispered, spinning to squint through the back windshield. "Cops."

I swiveled in my seat and peeked, blinded by the sun reflecting off the glass. The black-and-white sedan was a ways away but gaining on us, and I'd always heard that's not a good thing.

"What are you doing?" I whispered, feeling the car shift.

"I'm pulling over."

"What?! Why?!"

"I'm letting them pass."

"What if they're not passing us?!" I whined as our tires slowed.

"Keep your head," he replied, glancing into his rear-view mirror every other second.

"Cliff . . ." I squirmed in my seat, watching the patrol car close in on us. "Cliff, they're right on our—"

"Keep your *fucking* head," he whispered sternly, putting the car in park.

I closed my eyes and waited, but for what, I didn't know. Maybe sirens? A knock on my window? A disturbance in the natural stability of the slope to my right? A mudslide didn't seem like the worst scenario ever.

I slowly blinked my way back to the car, steeling myself for whatever was coming to me. But to my surprise, the sedan cruised by and took a left turn into BC's driveway.

A couple who'd been standing beside their station wagon met the officers on the lawn. My eyes shot to the back of their car where a tent, duffle bags, and coolers were stacked high to the ceiling, and suddenly, the non-existent police report made a lot more sense.

Why would we ever vow to stay silent? Because sometimes words aren't necessary. And when you're watching the parents of the girl you dumped in the woods report coming home to a daughterless house, they're practically senseless.

6 KINDNESS

Kindness: A simple act of human decency. The very thing that proves not everyone has a wrong side to their bed. A sweet text. A returned lost wallet. A compliment while standing in the grocery line. They say you'll never forget these gestures, that they're so touching, nothing can strip you of the high you feel when you experience them. *Nothing*, however, is a very strong word. And by the end of that day, it would prove to be the wrong one.

My feet smacked against the track like bricks, and I questioned the sanity of whoever said running relieves stress. I was on lap two and none the calmer. If anything, jogging around the football field gave me time to relive the previous morning's happenings.

I knew it was coming, I just didn't expect it to leak to Westcott overnight. Whispers of a missing girl were in every conversation, and no matter how quickly I ran, I couldn't escape them.

Up ahead, I saw Kyle drop to the bleachers and lift his sneaker over one knee, digging into the soles before chucking something clear across the track. I ran some more then kneeled to pick up the mystery item.

"I think you dropped your Lego."

He lifted his head, squinting to keep the sun out of his eyes as I dropped the block in his hand. "Aren't you supposed to be running?"

"Aren't you?"

"I finished," he replied, staring at me like the kid who got picked last in volleyball.

"Oh." With my hands on my hips and my chest pumping out of my shirt, I glanced across the turf. "I've got one lap on Winston, so I've got time."

"One and a half," he replied, scooting over as I dropped beside him. Things between us were shaky at best, but I was making every effort to steer things back to normal.

"So? What gives?"

"Nothing," he replied.

"Come on, Ky. I know you. I even knew you were going to say that."

"Did you want a cookie?"

"Ask me again in two more laps," I quipped, pushing him on the knee. "Seriously, what's up?"

He paused, and I wish I could've seen what he was thinking, because I knew whatever he was about to say would only be half-true. "I'm just overwhelmed with this Casey stuff."

"Casey stuff? You mean her moving in?" Our conversation from the bakery came to mind, and the statement he made about making a mistake rang true. I slowly nodded as it hit me. "You regret it, don't you?"

Kyle glanced my way. "I don't regret her getting the help she needed. I just question if *I* should have been the one to offer it."

"Where is this coming from?" I asked.

Kyle glanced down at the Lego in his palm. "I guess I'm just having a hard time adjusting to the new setup."

"You're an only child, Ky. That would be hard for anyone in your shoes."

As Winston flapped by like a bird missing a wing, I knew I was running out of time to uncover the real reason for Kyle's saddened state. "We can sit here and talk about half-inch plastic cubes if you'd like, but I think we both know what you're truly mad about."

His eyes shot a question mark to the side of my face.

"Sawyer," I continued. "He threatened to take away his offer to help Casey and her brothers, so you stepped in and saved the day. Now he's trotting around your house like he owns the place, and Casey is none the wiser."

Kyle shrugged. "She can do what she wants."

"Pretending you don't care will only result in more injured Legos."

"Look—I care, but what can I do?"

"You can tell her the truth!" I exclaimed. "That he was only going to help them if you turned on Cliff."

"I can't."

"Why not?"

"Because that will hurt her," he replied.

"Yeah, well, so would finding out you knew but didn't say anything."

Kyle shook his head. "I'm not going to be the reason she breaks it off with him. She has to come to that decision on her own . . . or not."

His words forced my head lower as I thought about Casey, and Sawyer, and Casey and Sawyer together, and just how terrible it would be if she never came to that decision.

A vibration in my running shorts' pocket drug me out of my thoughts. I reached in and grabbed my cell, and my heart dropped as soon as my eyes hit the screen.

"You gonna go?"

I glanced at Kyle then locked my phone and sandwiched it between my hands. "Hasn't anyone ever told you it's rude to read people's texts?"

"Hasn't anyone ever told you it's rude to answer a question with a question?"

I rolled my eyes. "Look, why are you even asking me? It's not like I have a choice."

"What do you mean?"

"I mean, I can't avoid him like I hoped. Not anymore. Not after—" I glanced behind my shoulder at the row of empty bleachers. "Any minute now, Jacob's going to realize this missing girl from the next town over is his ex. If I act like something's up, he could think I figured that out."

"So?"

"So he could think I had something to do with her disappearance."

"You honestly think Jacob will believe you had something to do with—" Kyle paused then swallowed the rest of his sentence. "So what have you been doing?" he asked, trying to bury the awkwardness. "Just pretending everything's fine between you two?"

"Essentially." I rubbed my lips, recalling our kiss. "I'm going to try to hold him off and blame it on not being over Dean, but I don't know how long that'll work."

"You need an out . . ."

"Yeah." I nodded. "One that's not going to furrow any brows."

Kyle caught an incoming football and tossed it back to his newly arrived buddy. "Maybe he'll tell you the truth."

"Huh?"

"Maybe once he realizes his ex has been here this entire time, it'll click that she was the one doing all that shit to you. Maybe he'll feel responsible and fess up." He caught another ball to the gut. "You can break things off with him for lying."

"And what if he doesn't come clean? What then?"

Kyle pushed himself off the bleacher and joined his friend on the field. "Like I said before . . . I don't have all the answers!"

"Ky!" I shouted, lunging forward. "Ky, come back here!"

Suddenly, I was knocked to the ground by an approaching jogger, and my phone went flying across the asphalt.

"Sorry!"

I pushed myself off my stomach and stood, watching as the runner bent down to retrieve my cell. "No problem," I replied, widening my eyes just briefly before they narrowed.

Guy Penn stood before me, his hand dangling between us while he held my gaze. His brown curls laid wet across his forehead, and his cheeks were redder than the crimson shirt sticking to his chest.

"Thanks . . ." I mumbled, taking my phone from his fingers.

He studied me for a moment longer before turning his head and sprinting off.

Sure, stranger things have happened during gym class. But Guy Penn walking away from an opportunity to deliver a creepy one-liner was high on the list—just high enough to raise concern.

"Hi, you." Jacob stood in his foyer holding the edge of the door in his hand. His biceps were hiding underneath his long-sleeved cream shirt, and his face was glowing.

"Are you—" I squinted. "Are you wearing moisturizer?"

He tapped his forehead and smiled. "Steam. From the spaghetti."

"You're cooking?"

"Of course," he replied, staring me up and down and opening the door wider. "When I invite you to dinner, that's sort of implied."

"I figured you'd order something."

"Really? Don't take me for a chef?"

"Didn't say that." I stepped inside and kicked my boots off then tucked my black shirt into my black jeans. For obvious reasons, black had been a frequent color choice that week.

Jacob closed the front door and led me to the kitchen. A pot sat on every burner, white plates were stacked on the island, and the smell of tomato sauce and garlic permeated the air.

"Didn't know you were going all out."

"Is that what this is?" He placed a sheet of garlic bread on a dish towel in front of me then turned to drain the pasta.

"Can I do anything to help?" I asked.

"Absolutely not."

"Don't trust me?"

"Implicitly," he replied. "But everything's done."

I stared at the back of his head while he stirred the meat sauce, watching as his muscles moved beneath his fitted shirt. "Implicitly," I muttered. "That's a big word."

"Is it?"

"Unquestionably."

"Ah." He nodded. "I see you're challenging me to a word battle."

A small smile crept to my lips, but I quickly caught it and chucked it. "You, um, you cook a lot?"

"Only for really pretty girls," he replied, joining me at the table with two bowls full of spaghetti. "I made an exception for you."

"Must've," I replied. "May I?"

He dared me with his eyes, watching as I twirled the noodles around my fork. I lifted it toward my lips and felt a warmth I hadn't felt in days. "Wow. You must know a lot of pretty girls."

"Just one. But I do cook a lot, if that's what you're implying."

I nodded, breaking my garlic bread in two. "Ever tackled a Vietnamese dish?"

"Sadly, no. Got any suggestions for me?"

"*Oh*!" I sighed at the thought. "My dad makes the best *Chè Ba Màu*—a three-colored dessert with the tastiest coconut sauce you'll ever have in your life."

"Your *dad*?" He squinted. "I'm skeptical . . ."

"I swear! It was the dessert they had on their first date. And by date, I mean family dinner at the Phan household because my grandparents were so strict, they wouldn't allow my mom to see anyone."

"Hang on—" He beamed from ear to ear. "Your parents were high school sweethearts?"

"Magical, huh?"

"Something like that," he answered, his doubt petering out. "Wait, so what happened? During the date?"

"Oh, nothing. My grandfather watched my dad like a hawk the entire night. It was incredibly awkward and all-around disheartening for him."

"I can imagine . . ."

"He swore that as soon as he could, he'd have her over for dinner and make his own version of *Chè Ba Màu*. Been making it ever since."

Jacob smiled. "Well, I'd love to try it sometime. Maybe you could teach me how to make it."

"Sure! I'd love—" Suddenly, I caught a glimpse of my reflection in the window behind Jacob. It was hazy but clear enough for me to see I'd been swept away by him. Allowed myself to have an effortless conversation with him. We'd smiled and laughed and shared stories about my grandfather and coconut sauce.

For a moment, I'd forgotten who he was. For a second, I wished I could enjoy him again. And for the life of me, I couldn't tell which was more concerning.

"You okay?" he asked, gently placing his hand on top of my wrist.

"Yeah." I pulled away. "Yeah, just tired."

"You wanna go lie down?"

"Oh, I, um . . . I don't know."

"I promise to set an alarm this time," he joked. "You have my word."

Memories of our first sleepover came to mind, and knowing BC was standing outside taking photos of us made the hair on my neck stand up.

"Come on," he nudged. "We can save this for later and go hang in my room."

I shouldn't have agreed, but my tired body gave in to his suggestion. I waited shamefully in the corner of the kitchen while Jacob rinsed the pots and covered our food. A few rips of foil later, he tossed a paper towel into the trash can as if it were a basketball then stretched his hand out for me to take.

And I did.

He led me up the stairs, and Ron's voice echoed down the hall. An orange glow peeked out from underneath his office door, and I almost wished I were heading in there to talk about Farrah Klein instead of trotting toward his son's bedroom.

"Lights out or movie?" he asked after he'd closed the door behind us.

"Movie's fine," I slurred, pinching the bridge of my nose and plopping down on his bed. His fluffy comforter could've swallowed me whole, and I wouldn't have cared. My body ached, and I knew all the sleepless nights were catching up to me. "Do you have any medicine?"

"Headache?" he asked, glancing back at me while scrolling through Netflix.

I nodded, and he opened his dresser drawer. "I'm sorry you don't feel good. I wish I would've picked a better night to have you over."

"Tonight's a good night," I replied, taking the meds from his palm.

"There's a water bottle on the nightstand."

I reached over and grabbed it, exposing mint-julep-and-jade-striped paper underneath. It caught my eye. I'd never seen that color combination before, and I was almost jealous I didn't own something so unique.

Curiosity got the better of me. I lifted it to my face, and my eyes narrowed as the chicken scratch before me seemed to form some sort of love note. I scrambled to make sense of it but didn't get very far before Jacob snatched the letter from my fingers.

"You want something to wear?" he asked, folding the letter in half.

"No." I swallowed the pills. "No, I'm okay."

Jacob picked a pair of sweats from the pile on his beanbag chair, cleverly taking the paper with him as he disappeared behind his bathroom door. When he reentered the room, he was shirtless like it didn't even matter.

His gray joggers hugged his ankles and sat snug around his waist, and when he ran his hand through his shaggy brown hair, his strange behavior seemed insignificant.

He killed the light and hopped into bed, pulling the cover over his chest. "Come here," he whispered, lifting the corner.

I climbed in, and warm, mossy notes lingered on his sheets. He pulled me toward him, keeping his hands high.

"Is this okay?"

"Yeah, I, um—"

"I'm not going to try anything," he said. "I promise."

"I know, it's just—"

"What?" He had patience in his eyes but not a lot. I could tell having to wait was wearing on him. "What's wrong?"

I shrugged, hoping he'd pick up what I was putting down. Unfortunately for me, he wanted answers.

"I can't hug you?"

"You can . . ."

"But not hold you?" he asked, trying to understand the rules that didn't exist. "What's the difference?"

I dropped my head.

"Sorry." Jacob squeezed his eyes shut. "I didn't mean for it to sound like that, I just—" He paused. "If there's a difference, that's fine; I just need you to tell me."

Don't act weird, Sonny. Blame it on Dean . . . blame it all on Dean.

"It's just—you know—I'm not ready."

Jacob's eyes became heavy, like he understood but didn't really in the slightest. Given our recent string of texts, maybe he thought we were making progress. Maybe he thought the next time we hung out, we'd be closer, not further, from the finish line. "Yeah." He nodded, obviously disappointed that he was wrong. "Yeah, okay. Get some rest."

He turned on his back and pressed play on the remote while I curled myself into a ball of shame. The words coming from the television drifted further and further into the distance, and within minutes, my eyes failed me.

When I opened them again, I was *really* going to wish that comforter had swallowed me whole.

"Sonny? Sonny, wake up."

I groaned and rolled over. Jacob was sitting on the edge of the mattress, staring down at me.

"It's eleven," he whispered. "You should probably head home soon."

I took a deep breath and pulled my body toward the headboard. "Guess I fell asleep?"

"Yeah," he replied, his voice raspy and rather attractive. "Three minutes in."

"Did you finish the movie?"

"I did."

"That's good," I said, lifting my arms in a stretch. "I didn't know you liked sci-fi."

He paused. "I, uh . . . I didn't know you talked in your sleep."

"Oh, only when I'm really drained." I wiped the dry mascara off my cheeks. "Hope I didn't say anything embarrassing. I didn't . . . did I?"

"We don't have to talk about that." He tucked his chin, staring down at his carpet for what seemed like minutes. With a deep sigh, he looked up and stared out into his room. "But we do need to talk."

Kindness: A simple act of human decency. A fed parking meter. A held elevator door. The gentle swipe of a hand that wakes you so you don't miss curfew. Experiencing these moments send you on a high, a high that no person or thing can disturb. Nothing apart from hearing those four little words everyone dreads hearing. That, my friends, is extremely unsettling.

7 SURPRISES

Not all surprises are good ones. Sometimes, they come in the form of things you never even wanted. Like a fortieth birthday party when you wished to stay thirty-nine or a free baked good with your morning coffee when you swore you were starting your diet. In fact, you don't know a bad surprise until you've had a strawberry frosted donut shoved in your face after guzzling down carrot juice.

But there *are* surprises that take you off guard in the best possible way. Like receiving gifts you always knew you wanted . . . or forming friendships with people you never knew you needed.

"*Us*?"

The room was pitch-black, but I wasn't complaining. Had he seen the horror etched across my face, I wouldn't have been able to pretend that I didn't know what he was talking about.

"Yeah." Jacob reached over and turned on his lamp, squinting at the brightness. He stared at me too long for my liking, and all I could do was wait. "I think we should be honest about what's going on here."

"What do you mean?"

"This." He stood to his feet and waved his hand back and forth between us. "It's clearly going nowhere."

"Going *nowhere*?"

He folded his arms across his bare chest and shrugged. "I've been bending over backward trying to prove myself to you. I drop everything I'm doing when you text me. I go out of my way to see you. I—I treat you with kid gloves just so I don't go too fast or cross any lines, but for what? You're nowhere near being ready for a relationship."

"That's not true . . ."

"How is it not true, Sonny? You do nothing to show me you're still interested in me."

"What are you talking about? I'm here right now!"

"Barely!"

"That is *not* fair." I shot out of bed. "You don't get to shame me, Jacob. Look, yes, I needed time to figure everything out. I needed time to heal from Dean, and I wasn't ready to jump right back into something new, but that doesn't mean I wasn't trying."

“Needed or need?”

“What?”

“You needed time, and I understood that—I gave you that—but I’ve got to be honest with you, Sonny, if you still aren’t sure about me, I don’t know if time is the problem here.”

“Seriously?” I huffed. “I gave up *everything* for you, and you’re going to scold me for not being quick enough?”

“Quite the opposite.” He shook his head. “I’m not going to do anything anymore.”

My eyes softened.

“Dean’s a decent guy,” he continued. “It’s obvious he loves you, and I know you love him. You two should fix things.”

“Jacob—”

“You’ve been acting weird toward me for weeks. You pull away every time I touch you. You couldn’t even kiss me on the trampoline without bursting into tears.”

“No, you don’t understand, I—”

“I could wait if I knew I was going to get what I was waiting for, but it’s obvious I’m not. You’re still in love with Dean.”

“Wait, what?”

“I’m done, Sonny.” He must have been devastated to have to say those two words before hearing the three he’d been holding out for. I suppose the way he choked on my name confirmed that.

"Jacob—" I tried again, though I wasn't sure why. He was giving me my out—an even better out than I could have hoped for—so why wasn't I taking it and running for the hills?

"You should leave," he said, giving me a push.

"*What*?"

"You should go," he replied.

My heart dropped when I realized he hadn't misspoken.

"Come on." He reached for a hoodie. "There's a girl missing from Jefferson . . . I want to walk you out."

As I approached the glass front door, I couldn't help but think it was wider than I remembered, though I'm sure the surrounding full-height windows contributed to that. I stepped onto the white slab they called a porch and rang the bell, wondering if anyone had ever told them that five motion-censored lights was rather excessive.

"Sonny?"

"Hi, Mr. Reynolds." I wiped my cheeks and forced a smile. "Is Cliff home?"

"Yes . . ." He tightened his house coat. "May I ask what you're doing here at ten thirty on a school night?"

"Are you asking . . . ?"

He peered at me.

"It's just that—" I gulped. "It's just that your question seemed more like a statement."

"A what?"

"You know, like passive aggressive?"

He crossed his arms. "Passive aggressive?"

"Often compared to its synonym 'snide' . . . ?"

Mr. Reynolds stared at me like I'd just walked off my spaceship. "I'm sorry; what the hell are we talking about here?"

"*Dad*?"

He whipped around to find Cliff slowly walking toward us. His head bounced back and forth between his son and the crazy girl standing on his porch, and eventually, he checked out. "Just lock up when you're done," he sighed, patting Cliff on the shoulder before heading back to bed.

Cliff waited until he was out of sight then shut us outside beneath the spotlights. "What are you doing here?"

"Picking you up."

"Okay?" His eyes did a lap around the yard. "For?"

"Coffee."

My mouth met the porcelain white mug, and I took in the warm liquid like it was the remedy I'd been missing. The tea swam through my body, and the taste of honey lingered on my lips as I lowered the cup and glared across the table at Piper.

“What do you want this time?” she asked, her hair tossed back in a messy ponytail like she’d just rolled out of bed. Technically speaking, I suppose she had.

“Information,” I replied, glancing at Ashley while she served a customer some joe. Going to Geraldine’s after everything we knew seemed wrong, but it was the only twenty-four-hour coffee shop in town, and our ten-dollar order wasn’t going to make or break them.

“Information, that’s it?” Piper crossed her arms, clearly not ready to let bygones be bygones. “Not my firstborn child?”

“Step off your perch, Clemmons. You’ve done much worse.”

“And that is *exactly* why I tell Ari not to pursue you,” she replied. “You honestly think what I’ve done is worse than what the two of you did the other night? You’re twisted, Cliff.”

“And you’re . . . ?”

“Not you.”

He smirked. He nodded. He dropped his smile and lifted his chin. “Don’t ever tell Ari some stupid shit like that again. You don’t know anything about me.”

Piper tried to hold his gaze, but apparently she wasn’t quite built for that kind of confrontation. With tears forming, she turned toward me. “What information do you need?”

“I, um—” I shook off their heated exchange. “I need you to tell me what you know about BC.”

"You can't be serious." Piper huffed. "You dragged me out of bed to talk about *this*? *Here*?"

"It's important."

"What could be so important?"

"Jacob doesn't know her," I replied.

Piper's eyes narrowed. "But I thought you said—"

"He referred to her as a 'missing girl from Jefferson.'" I shrugged. "She wasn't his ex."

"And you believe him?"

"Yeah." I nodded, recalling the casualness of his voice. "I do."

"I don't," Cliff added. "Not yet. And even if he doesn't know her, she knew him, and we need to know why she was pretending to be Claire."

"What for?" Piper asked, hesitant to look his way. "The girl's dead. Does it even matter?"

"Yes, it matters," Cliff groaned. "We need to know who we're dealing with."

"Who we *were* dealing with."

"Look, just—" He pinched the bridge of his nose. "Just *think*, Clemmons. Did she ever talk about anyone? Anyone who could know that she knew Sonny?"

"Not that I recall . . ."

"What *can* you tell us about her?" I asked.

"Not much." Piper leaned back with a sigh. "We were casual friends."

"How casual?"

"Casual, casual," Piper quipped. "She gave me pills, but other than that . . ."

"You never talked about anything?"

"Nothing serious."

"Home life? School?"

"I wish I could help, but we weren't that close." Piper wrapped her fingers around her coffee cup, Band-Aids on two, bruises on one. She took a swig, and her head tipped back as if she'd stumbled upon a hidden memory. "Harriet . . ."

I glanced at Cliff.

"She talked about visiting someone named Harriet once . . ."

"Harriet Lange?" he asked.

"Yeah, that sounds right." Piper nodded. "You know her?"

"That's not a person . . . it's a place." He fell back against his houndstooth chair. "My dad's buddy lives right around the corner from it. It's a mental health facility."

"That could explain her access to pills . . ." Piper trailed off. "Maybe she was a patient there."

Just then, the coffee-shop door flew open, and a gaggle of Cliff's football friends walked in. He lifted his chin their way as Piper stood to her feet. "Anything else?"

"No." My eyes did a lap across her body. "Thanks."

She grabbed her coat and stalked toward the door, leaving me and Cliff alone in our confusion.

"God, I can't believe I ruined my relationship with Jacob over nothing!" I dropped my forehead on the table not nearly as hard as I should have. "How could I be so stupid?"

"It's not your fault," Cliff replied. "The girl told you she was Claire."

"Why'd I have to bring Dean into this?" I griped. "Why? *Why*?"

"That I don't get."

"Jacob kissed me," I explained. "I freaked, and I needed a reason."

"And you thought Dean was a good reason?"

"It made sense, okay?" I slowly lifted my head, staring at my reflection in the large glass window. "Until now."

"Look, you'll fix it." Cliff wasn't the type of guy to sit around and talk about feelings, so the longer I spoke, the more impatient he became. "Just go home and get some rest."

I yawned as if his words gave me permission to be tired. "Come on. I'll drive you back to your place."

"Don't worry about it," he replied, glancing at his buddies. "I'll catch a ride with them."

"You sure?"

Cliff nodded then scanned me up and down. If my eyes weren't playing tricks on me, I could've sworn I saw an ounce of consideration in his. "Drive safe."

He tapped the table with his knuckle twice before drifting toward the other side of the room. I couldn't understand why, but from the moment he left, I really wished he wouldn't have.

Some surprises take you off guard in the best possible way. Like forming friendships with people you never knew you needed . . . and never knew you wanted.

8 LOOSE LIPS

Loose lips sink ships. An old World War II slogan that still rings true today. It goes without saying that unguarded talk may give your enemy useful information, and in a town like Westcott, it could mean your demise.

You see, discretion is the key to staying afloat . . . well, part of it.

"What kind of name is 'Harriet'?" Winston asked, walking beside me through the parking lot the following morning. I'd just filled him in on the news, and not surprisingly, he didn't exactly care. "Did I tell you my mother almost named me Freemore?"

"You did not . . ."

"She copped to that during one of her sleep-talking episodes," he replied. "Right after confessing to burying our pet goldfish, Henry, in the rose garden. Except we didn't have a pet goldfish . . . or a rose garden . . . and Henry was our cat . . . who also disappeared . . ."

"Winston?" I snapped my fingers. "Come back."

He blinked then peeled the liner on his red velvet cupcake. "So you think Jacob's telling the truth?"

"For once? Yes." I opened the door to the school and stepped inside. "You should have seen his face when he said 'missing girl.' It was completely blank. He doesn't know her."

"Didn't."

Winston and I gave each other a pained look before I pretended he'd never said that. "Now I just have to figure out why she was impersonating Claire."

"Maybe the girl was just off her rocker," Winston mumbled through a mouthful of cake. "She did go to Henrietta Lake."

"*Harriet Lange*. And that's borderline insensitive."

"It's extremely insensitive."

I rolled my eyes, trying to get back on track. "That night in the parking lot, when I told her I knew who she was . . . she asked me if I pieced it all together."

"So?"

"So that means there was something to piece together," I replied. "And it wasn't that she was Claire like I assumed."

"And you're sure you believe Jacob?"

I nodded. "Not that it matters anymore . . ."

"Who would've guessed your plan to delay things with him would backfire?" Winston shrugged. "In retrospect, I guess it makes sense."

"You guess?" I exhaled. "God, Wins, everything is so screwed up."

"He really told you he was done?"

"Walked me to my car and everything."

Winston tossed the end of his blue-and-gray-checkered scarf over his shoulder. "In the olden days, they called that 'getting the boot.'"

"Oh, yeah?"

He nodded.

"What a coincidence. I'd like to shove my boot straight up your—"

"Sonny!"

My sneakers squeaked against the tile as I turned around.

"A word?" Mr. Harrison lifted a brow, waiting for me to meet him at the other end of the hall.

"I think he wants to have a word with you," Winston mumbled.

"Yeah, I got that, Winston, thanks." I let out a deep breath. "What do you think he wants?"

"*A word*?"

"I'll be right back," I mumbled, jostling my way through the crowd in pursuit of Mr. Harrison. "I have class in five minutes," I told him, coming to a halt.

"Great," he replied. "This will only take three."

I tucked my hands into my back pockets and nodded.

"The Princeton profile—you mentioned Mr. Russell gave that to you, yes?"

"Um . . ."

"At least, I think that's what you said," he continued. "If we're being technical, Principal Winchester said it, and you agreed. Correct?"

"Yeah," I mumbled. "That's correct."

"You know, Sonny, I just can't seem to wrap my head around that." Ron bit down on the inside of his cheek and dropped his head. "It's no secret certain people have pull at certain colleges. There are some people who seem to have pull with everyone everywhere. I'm sure you know that by now."

I shrugged. "Hierarchy at its finest."

"Exactly," he replied, a tiny grin appearing. "And it's no surprise someone here at Westcott had that kind of pull with the Admissions Department at Princeton, would you agree?"

"I would."

"You would." He nodded. "Would you also agree that the chances of that person being a fifty-eight-year-old, unmarried, TV-dinner-eating English teacher making less than 80k a year would be slim to none?"

My heart dropped.

"Seems unlikely, no? Seems like you would've had to be a bit more important to get your hands on something like that."

"He was alumnus," I recited, unable to think of a better response.

"So you wouldn't agree?"

"I—I mean, I—"

"You would?"

"Well, no, I—"

"You what?" He tilted his head. "You also find it strange that someone on the bottom tier could swing that transaction?"

"I—"

"I need you to do two things for me," he interjected, stepping closer and lowering his voice to a mumble. "In your own words, I need you to tell me how Mr. Russell got his hands on that list, and then I need to know why he would ever hand it over to someone who had absolutely zero interest in Princeton."

Just then, the bell rang, and students began emptying the halls to pack into classrooms like sardines.

"I'll give you a few days, yeah?" He patted me on the back and pushed against the flow of traffic toward his office.

"What did he want?" Winston asked as he returned to my side.

I peered down the hall just in time to catch the tail end of Ron's slacks disappear behind the adjacent wall. "Something I can't give him."

"Alright, students, take your seats!"

I dragged my feet toward my desk, dreading the next hour and a half with fierceness. Communications was already one of my least favorite blocks, but knowing I had to stare at the back of Dean's head for the duration of the class sealed the deal.

I dropped into my seat, not bothering to glance at Dean along the way. I knew he wasn't looking at me. In fact, he'd been making a point not to. Months prior, he was pleading for a second chance. Weeks prior, he was attempting to make things right with the likes of a dozen roses and a nice suit. But on that day, in that classroom, he was nothing but a stranger wearing joggers and a five o'clock shadow.

"Today, class, we'll be having a conversation about the emotional and psychological impact that sudden loss has on your life." Mr. Rochester was no Mr. Russell, but if I had to turn to someone with my problems, he made the most sense. He was an eccentric little guy—five-foot-six with shaggy black hair, yellow glasses, and the personality of a bona fide underdog. It was almost as if he enjoyed making everyone else feel superior. Luckily for him, everyone already did.

"Alright, now, has anybody in this room ever suffered a loss?" He leaned against his desk and peered into the classroom, his arms folded high. "Maybe it was sudden, or maybe you knew it was coming—and please, don't everybody volunteer at once."

A chuckle broke out across the room, and a few people cleared their throats. I couldn't blame any of my classmates for their reluctance to speak up—death wasn't exactly a fun topic to discuss with a group of people you didn't trust.

"Anyone?" he tried again. After another long and painful pause, Dean slowly lifted his finger in the air.

"Ah! Mr. Ballinger! Please, join me." Mr. Rochester extended his palm toward the right side of his desk, prompting Dean to roll out of his. "Anyone else?"

"Uh, yes, sir!" I swiveled in my chair to find Guy pushing to his feet. His beige waffle Henley shirt matched his sandy-colored beanie, and his curly brown hair had a mind of its own that morning. "Unfortunately, I have."

"Mr. Penn!"

Guy put one Vans in front of the other and glided toward the chalkboard. His jeans had more holes in them than our friend group, and the little roll at the bottom of his pant legs made him seem a tad less terrifying than normal. He stood on the left side of the desk, tucked his hands into his pockets, and immediately locked eyes with me.

"Now, as we've discussed in the past, sudden loss brings upon immediate change and demands adjustment. People who have experienced this may feel a range of emotions. Despair, anger, loneliness." Mr. Rochester glanced at both boys. "Why don't the two of you come forward and face each other?"

Regret was written across Dean's face, and I knew he wished he'd never raised his hand. Dragging his feet, he inched his way toward the center of the classroom where Guy was waiting.

"Let's try a little exercise here," Mr. Rochester continued, placing his hands on each of their shoulders. "Dean, I know you lost your mom not too long ago, and if you're comfortable with sharing, why don't you tell Guy the impact that's had on your life."

Guy widened his stance and crossed his arms, his body language screaming trouble. I grabbed the sides of my desk, hoping Dean could hear the sirens going off in my head, begging him to feel my energy from so many feet away. Something wasn't right.

"Just, uh—" Dean shrugged. "Just been tough without her here."

"Tough, yes, yes." Mr. Rochester nodded. "How so?"

"I don't know . . . just tough."

"Care to elaborate?" he asked.

Dean dragged his eyes back to Guy. I could tell he actually *didn't* care to elaborate—not to Guy, anyway. "I guess I just miss talking to her when something good happens." He rolled his shoulders back and stood a little taller, holding Guy's gaze. "It sucks knowing she'll never know me past fifteen.

She won't get to see me graduate or go to college or get married. She won't ever get to see me again, and I'll never get to see her." He shrugged. "Like I said . . . just tough."

Mr. Rochester cleared his throat. "Could one assume it's changed the way you interact with people on a day-to-day basis?"

Dean shrugged again, which inadvertently answered his question.

"Perhaps you find it difficult to be vulnerable?"

"Sure."

"You may struggle with letting people get close to you?"

"Yep."

"And why do you think that is, Mr. Ballinger?"

"Subconsciously, I probably assume they'll leave me, too," he coolly replied.

Mr. Rochester scooted them closer. "And if that were to happen, tell Mr. Penn here how that would affect you."

"It wouldn't," Dean replied.

Guy smirked.

"Well, that's perfectly understandable, my friend. Sometimes it's easier to put up walls rather than feel what we're feeling." He turned to the class. "At times, it may seem easier to restrict yourself from feeling anything at all. But studies show that suppressing your emotions can lead to stress on your body, which could bring on multiple health issues.

Avoiding emotions may lead to problems with depression, anxiety, even aggression."

"That's a good thing to have on the court," a basketball player shouted from the back of the room.

"That may be," Mr. Rochester replied, speaking loudly over the scattered laughter. "And it can certainly help you win ball games, but learning how to process loss far outweighs those temporary benefits. Talking to friends like we've done here today is necessary for healing. Would you agree, Mr. Penn?"

Guy raised his brows. "Oh, definitely. And I'm sorry to hear about your mother, Dean." The room grew quiet as Guy steered the conversation back toward *Heavyville*. "My mom means everything to me, and life without her would be meaningless. I just—I just can't imagine it."

Weeks prior, Mrs. Penn was a nutjob who threw his clothes into trash bags when he didn't clean his room, but suddenly, she was his everything?

"Aside from losing a child, I can't imagine anything more difficult than losing a parent," Guy continued. "I still have mine, thank God, but I did lose someone very special to me. A friend."

Mr. Rochester tilted his head.

"A best friend, really. The only one I had."

"Well, I'm very sorry to hear that, Guy."

"Yeah," he replied, unyielding in his eye contact with Dean. "Me, too."

"You know, Mr. Penn, the death of a friend can be just as traumatizing as that of a loved one. In fact, studies show—"

"Oh, she isn't dead."

Mr. Rochester blinked. "She isn't?"

"No." Guy's malicious grin squeezed the life out of the room. "*She's missing*."

I teetered on the edge of my desk, my depth perception gone. I felt like I'd been leaning forward for minutes, like I was sitting on a conveyer belt on the slow track to calamity.

"Guy, are you referring to the girl from Jefferson?"

"Yes, sir," he replied. "No one's seen her in over a week."

"That's, uh—" Dean tucked his chin, slowly tilting his head until our eyes met. "That's pretty unfortunate."

"Very," Guy replied. "But the police are involved now, so I'm hoping they'll find her soon."

"I'm sure they will." Mr. Rochester patted his shoulder. "Dean, maybe you could offer Guy some comforting words?"

He straightened his head, and I prayed to all things holy that his facial hair masked his cherry-red cheeks. "I'm, uh, I'm not sure what to say."

"Anything works," Guy replied.

My heart was beating out of my chest, but I hoped Dean's wasn't. *Play it cool*, I thought—and possibly mouthed—as I watched in agony.

“I’m, uh . . . I’m sure she’s fine.”

“Yeah.” Guy nodded, though nothing about his body language agreed with him. He removed his beanie and shook a hand through his hair, placing it back on his head before glaring at Dean. “She better be.”

Their prolonged eye contact became threatening, so much so that Mr. Rochester himself was slow to break it. He pushed himself off his desk and cleared his throat. “The class thanks you both for participating. You may take your seats.”

“Rochester?” Dean lifted his finger. “Bathroom?”

“Quickly, Mr. Ballinger.”

I watched Dean stalk toward the door with a sense of urgency then dropped my head as Guy walked by me. My mind raced for answers, but my hand shot in the air before I could find them. “Me, too.” Mr. Rochester glanced my way. “The, um, the bathroom . . . please?”

He sighed. “Go on, Ms. Carter.”

I scooted out of my desk, finding myself in the hallway before he could finish his sentence. How, out of the hundreds of kids at Westcott High, did BC manage to make friends with the two people we trusted least in this world?

“No,” I mumbled under my breath. “No, this can’t be happening.”

But it was, and it had—Guy Penn was back.

Halfway to the restroom, I was yanked by my forearm into a dimly lit nook.

"What are you—"

Dean put his finger over his lips, urging me to stay quiet. The sound of keys shaking echoed through the hall, and within seconds, the conversation between two men grew near. I looked up at him. He looked down at me. Our breathing paired as we stood there, pressed against each other for lack of space or concern.

He slowly released his grip, but his eyes held mine, demanding my silence while we waited for the voices to pass us. The closer they got, the closer we did.

My nose touched his gray cotton T-shirt, and I subtly snuck a whiff while I had the chance. The smell of Dean's cologne nearly brought me to my knees, and I exhaled into his chest as I closed my eyes. When I opened them and glanced up, he was staring down at me as if he knew I was breathing him in . . . as if he were allowing it.

Principal Clemmons and Ron Harrison passed by, but by then, they didn't seem to matter. We were caught in a force stronger than us—something more powerful than the damage four weeks of distance could do.

I knew Dean dragged me into that nook for a reason. I knew we should have talked about Guy and the serious insinuations he made regarding BC, but all we could do was stand there, stuck in a gaze neither of us could get out of.

I slowly lifted my hand and cupped his cheek; it was warm to the touch and as flushed as it could be. He clenched his jaw, allowing my hand to stay there but visibly frustrated by it—by us.

I wished I had the guts to walk out of his life instead of trying to convince him he didn't want to walk out of mine. Asking him to stay only served me, and I knew that. I knew it was wrong. I knew it was over between us . . . I guess I just didn't want him to hate me for it.

Dean grabbed my shoulders and slowly pushed them back—*me* back—and stared into my eyes with his arms stretched out. His jaw still clenched and his face still flushed, he dropped his hands and stepped out of the nook then strode back toward the classroom.

An hour or so after the final bell rang, I pulled into Kyle's driveway, eager to discuss the conversation from communications class. I also couldn't wait to verbally accost him for getting in the shower when I told him to hold off.

His text read *Door's open*, so I let myself inside. A large bouquet of Dracula simias sat in the center of the entryway table, and I made a mental note to ask Ms. Winchester why her favorite flowers looked like freaky little monkeys.

I kicked off my shoes before kneeling to smell one, unclear as to why. Maybe I wanted to feel human again, connect with something outside of myself. Bask in their sweet orange scent to remind me that not everything was as bad as it seemed.

"You know those are fake, right?"

I glanced to my right where Kyle stood towel-drying his chest at the bottom of the stairs.

"Yeah. Yeah, of course, I do," I replied, pulling my nose back from the plastic petal. "Listen, we have to talk."

"If this is about Jacob, I already know. Winston filled me in." Kyle glided toward the kitchen. Water from his shower dripped down his back, crashing into the waistband of his black sweats. "You believe him?"

"I do," I replied, following closely behind. "But that's not why I'm here."

"Oh, hell yes!" He reached for a fresh peanut butter cookie and sighed. "My mom is the literal best."

"Ky—"

"Want one?"

"No, thanks." My eyes narrowed. "Listen, I have to tell you what happened today."

Kyle reached into the fridge and grabbed the carton of milk then poured himself a glass.

"Hello?" I clapped my hands, wondering where his curiosity was. "Earth to my best friend?"

He lowered the cup and placed it on the counter, and with his back still to me, he hung his head. "You know what else Winston told me?"

"What?" I asked, by no means interested.

"He told me you were with Cliff last night."

My eyes instinctively closed, only opening again to search for the nearest knife to use on Winston.

"He, uh—" Kyle lifted his head and stared at the cabinet. "He told me you picked him up and went to Geraldine's together."

"Look, Ky, I can explain—"

"You drove by BC's together . . ." He turned. "Are you . . . Are you *together*?"

"What?!" I scrunched my entire face. "Are you out of your mind?!"

"No, Sonny. Just trying to figure out what could've made it worth it."

"Worth it? Worth what?"

"Losing me." Kyle stood like a statue, leaning against the counter before pushing himself forward to retrieve another cookie. "See yourself out," he mumbled, grabbing one before heading toward the steps.

"Ky!" I chased him. "Ky, just let me explain! Okay, yes, I've seen Cliff a few times, but it's not what it looks like. We're just trying to stay a few steps ahead of this!"

He picked up speed when he reached the living room, and not once did he turn around to engage.

"We aren't friends, okay? We're just colleagues if you think about it! We're just working together!" I ran forward to stop him from scaling the stairs, but the lime-green Legos up ahead had other plans for me. "*Shit*!" I fell to my knees, wincing in pain as I peeled a few of them off the bottom of my foot.

Kyle turned around, and our eyes met. I naively thought he'd feel as sorry for me as I did, but that didn't happen. "Go home, Sonny," he mumbled, staring at me like I was a nuisance. Just . . . *just go home*."

I watched him climb a few steps before I pushed to my feet. In one fell swoop, I cocked my arm and chucked the Legos straight at his back. My breathing quickened when he stopped in his tracks, and I stood there, going down with my pride like a captain with his ship. "Guy Penn is on to us," I hollered, a tear flying down my cheek as I pivoted toward the foyer. "Tell the others."

The Dracula simias rattled in their vase as I walked by, and before I had time to process what had happened, I was bawling into my steering wheel. Thank God it couldn't judge me for my hysterics—I'm sure I looked nasty.

My head fell back against my headrest when I saw the front door creep open. Hopeful it was Kyle, I wiped my eyes and sat up straight, only to narrow them and duck down when Casey and Sawyer emerged.

The way she paced beneath the porch light prompted me to crack my window, and I buried myself into the side of my door.

"We couldn't have talked inside?" he asked. "What's going on?"

Casey's eyes scanned left to right before lasering in on him. "There's something I need to tell you."

In a town like Westcott, discretion is the key to staying afloat . . . second to making sure everyone on your ship wants to.

9 ONE THING WORSE

I dread the end of chapters—in fictional worlds and in the real one. How many "just one more"s have I said while lost in a good book, pushing myself to finish, only to feel sad when I did? It's why we cry at graduations. It's why we mourn the friendships that fade throughout the years.

Reaching the end of a good thing just isn't natural, and if you ask me, there's nothing worse. Well . . . there's one thing worse.

"I need to talk to you."

The smell of something marvelous rushed to greet me at the door. It had to have been pasta of some kind, maybe baked ziti, and I was certain I smelled red wine on his breath.

"Okay?" Ron wiped his hands on a maroon dish towel then tossed it over his shoulder before stepping outside. I could tell my spontaneous visit wasn't appreciated. "This couldn't wait until the morning?"

"I'd rather not discuss this at school," I replied, my eyes shooting toward the welcome mat. A pair of Jacob's basketball shoes sat beside it, tugging at my heartstrings.

It's funny what objects can do to a person. In the split second it took to notice his dirty sneakers, I replayed our last conversation together and immediately missed him more than I cared to admit.

"This might be a stupid question, but is everything alright?"

"*Question*," I mumbled, dragging my eyes up to his. "I once came to you with questions about some suspicions I was having. You remember?"

"Of course."

"And I asked you what I should do if I had incriminating information about someone at my school . . ."

"Yes, I remember that well," he replied.

"But I never told you what." I wrapped myself into my jean jacket, gripping my elbows and holding back tears. "Because I can't tell you, Mr. Harrison. Because this is Westcott. This is a prestigious town, and I attend the top private school in the nation. Things happen behind those walls, things you wouldn't believe. But my job—my *only* job—is to excel academically and get into an ILS. It's what I've prepared for my entire life. It's the only thing that matters to me, and rest assured, I hate myself for that."

The first tear escaped, burning a track down my cheek. I wasn't sure if I was still upset about my fallout with Kyle or that realization, but it was probably a mixture of both. "If I've realized anything this year, it's that those tiers you mentioned are there for a reason. They aren't to be questioned, especially not by a bottom-of-the-totem-pole girl like me. If I want to survive the hierarchy, Mr. Harrison, then I have to fall in line like everyone else—keep my head down and my mouth shut."

"I see." Ron cleared his throat. "So you won't be answering my question then?"

"I'm a smart girl," I replied. "Smart enough to read between the lines. I realize what you're asking me to say about Mr. Russell and the profile, but I can't say it. And if you're as smart as I think you are, then you'll realize I just did."

At that moment, Jacob's Jeep pulled into the driveway. His headlights rolled across our bodies as we stood underneath the porch light. The sun was on its way down, but the sky wasn't dark yet, so the sudden urge to run and hide in the sagebrush bush made little sense.

"I'll let you get back to your dinner," I said softly, giving him no time to respond.

I felt a million pounds lighter after dropping that nugget into Ron's ear. With everything else going on, the last thing I needed was to open a can of worms I didn't have time to deal with. Maybe Ron had the time. Maybe, in time, he'd fight the war with Winchester for me.

My feet moved quickly through the lawn, but the sound of Jacob's car door opening stopped me in my tracks. I glanced to the left, still wrapped in my jacket and still heartbroken from our conversation the previous night.

Our eyes met. He sat in his car, just looking at me. I stood in his grass, just looking at him. Sadness hung between us like a curtain, the orange sky above moments away from trailing toward black.

I could see a basketball in his front seat, and his white T-shirt and gym shorts let me know he was down at the court shooting hoops.

He hopped out and leaned against the door, every movement he made slower than the last. Surprisingly, we held our gaze. I wasn't sure what I thought would happen next, but I didn't expect Jacob to head inside without saying a word.

I just stared, and I waited for him to come back with an offer to reconcile. But if the front door closing and the porch light turning off was any indication of where we stood, I realized that was never going to happen.

Early the next morning, I pulled open the heavy door of Laurel's Bakery. The holiday wreath was gone and replaced with a cheap plastic open sign—honestly, I welcomed it. December had been nothing but four weeks of pain, and though the new year was turning out to be worse, I didn't have to pretend to be jolly about it.

The previous twenty-four hours had led me straight to my bathtub the night before, where I devoured two pints of mint chocolate chip ice cream like it was my job. Between Guy, fighting with Kyle and Dean, and losing Jacob over a misunderstanding, I had unraveled, and the latest punch to the gut wasn't exactly helping.

"You look like shit," Cliff said as I took the seat across from him at the long wooden table. The shop was empty, as one would expect at six thirty in the morning.

I tightened my messy bun and served him a scowl. "High praise, Cliff, thanks."

He lifted his eyes to the barista. "Want something? Coffee?"

"A medium black would be great."

Cliff trailed toward the register and reached for his wallet. I stared down at the table, wondering how I was going to tell him the most recent news, wondering how, in just a few short weeks, he was all I had left.

Suddenly, his cell phone lit up. I glanced behind me at the counter then leaned over the screen. Ari's name flashed before me, and a paragraph full of legal jargon laid beneath it. But all the way at the bottom sat four little words, and they were far different than the ones Jacob had said to me days prior.

I love you, too disappeared just as Cliff reached for his phone. He handed me my coffee then dropped down in his seat and read the text.

It's not like I didn't know—everyone knew—but seeing it in writing changed things. It made it real . . . *confusing*.

How could Cliff claim to love Ari but not enough to be with her? How could he put himself on the line to clear her name but not want to cross the one he needed to cross to make it official?

Maybe Piper was right. Maybe Cliff was as twisted as she claimed.

"So what's going on?" he asked. "Do you have news on BC?"

"Not, um, not exactly." I removed my glasses and pressed my fingertips over my eyelids, my flannel shirt brushing my cheeks. I quickly realized I was wearing the same clothes I wore the last time he and I were at Laurel's together. So much had changed, and mostly for the worse—hence our second meeting in less than two days. "We have a problem . . . or two."

"Okay?"

"Guy Penn," I whispered, glancing left to right. "He knows."

"Knows what?"

"He knows I knew BC."

Cliff cupped his mouth, and his eyes left the table quicker than he'd returned to it.

"He announced his friend was missing in communications class yesterday then strongly insinuated he knew we had something to do with it."

"I thought you said Ky and JC were the only two people who knew that!"

"That's what I thought," I fired back. "You think if I had any idea Guy Penn was friends with BC, I would have agreed to your plan?"

Cliff shot to his feet, sending his metal chair flying. He started to walk away, but then he returned and placed his hands on top of the table, holding himself up but not together. "Who else knows this?"

"Dean." I blinked heavy eyes. "Kyle, too, and I told him to spread the news."

"What did he say?"

"Nothing," I replied. "We got into a fight before I could explain what happened in class."

"A fight? A fight about what?"

"*You.*" My response brought him back to his chair. "He asked me not to speak to you anymore, but he found out I have been. He doesn't understand why we're chasing after a dead girl . . . much less together."

"But you do, right?" Cliff's baby blues sucked me in. "This Guy shit is *exactly* why we're trying to stay two steps ahead."

"I know."

"We have to."

"*I know*," I replied.

Cliff fell back in his seat and shook his head. "God, he's such a little bitch."

"Cliff!"

"Asking you not to speak to me? Why? Because it hurts him?"

"Don't mock him." I lunged forward. "He's my best friend, and his feelings are valid."

"His feelings don't matter."

"How can you say that?"

"Because they have nothing to do with anything," he gritted. "You don't lead with your emotions at a time like this, you lead with your head. He can keep his buried in the sand if he wants to, that's fine, but we can't. We're responsible for what happens."

"I get it."

"Do you?"

"Of course, I do! Why do you think I'm here?! Why do you think I've been trying to figure this whole thing out?!"

"Stop filling him in," Cliff replied.

"What?"

"Stop filling Kyle in. Stop filling everyone in. From this point on, nobody gets to know shit unless it goes through me."

"Why not?"

"Because they're scared," he answered, his eyes blacker than my coffee. "They're better off oblivious."

I slid my frames back on and desperately tried pushing Kyle to the back of my mind. "Fine."

"I'm serious, Sonny."

"I said fine," I shot back, taking a deep breath to prepare myself for the next topic. "There's something else . . ."

Cliff squinted.

"At the end of last year, Sawyer threatened to retract his offer to help Casey and her brothers if Kyle didn't turn you in for . . . you know."

I could almost see the showcase play out across his eyes. They shot to mine and widened, waiting for more.

"Your little *bitch friend* wouldn't do it, which is why he offered up his home to them. The only way Ky got his mom to agree to it was by promising her he and Casey wouldn't cross any boundaries while under the same roof. So now, she's just doing that with Sawyer while Kyle's forced to watch." I lifted a brow. "He sacrificed a relationship with her to help you."

"Ky didn't tell her about Sawyer's threat?"

"That would break her heart," I replied. "He let her go instead."

Cliff's eyes descended to the tabletop. He was drowning in his cruel words, and I let him.

"Look, I know you might not care. I know you don't understand how Kyle could love someone like Casey, but for the life of me, I can't figure out why not. Sure, maybe she's a little *bluer* than Ari. Maybe her family isn't as normal. Depending on who you're asking, Ari may be just a tad bit cooler with her musical rifts and bad girl persona, but they're both Cobalts, Cliff. And you fell in love with one, too."

"You need to stop saying that."

"It's true."

"It's not, and it's none of your business."

"Cliff—"

"*It's none of your business*," he repeated, his eyes flashing. "God, what the hell is your problem? Why are you pushing me to admit I love that girl?"

"Because you do, and there's nothing wrong with that!"

"Since when?"

"I—"

"No, Sonny, since when?"

"I don't know!" I shouted. "I guess since I realized you deserve to be happy, too!"

Cliff allowed his eyes to soften, just a little.

"What you did to Kyle was horrible," I continued, "and that will never change. But denying yourself a relationship with Ari isn't fair punishment, it's torture."

"Look, even if I wanted it to, it wouldn't work."

"Why not?"

"Because."

"Because why?"

"Because I don't want to hurt her again!" he answered, angry I sucked that out of him. He looked down at tabletop and clenched his jaw. "What will happen if I do?"

"I don't know, Cliff. What will happen if you don't?" His eyes shot to mine as I stood to my feet. "Casey told Sawyer you're blackmailing her. I overheard their conversation yesterday at Kyle's. She didn't give him details—she wouldn't—she just told him to take care of her brothers if anything happened to her." I turned in the direction of the welcome mat. "We have to get to her before he gets her to talk. Call a meeting."

"I knew you could wrestle, but I had no idea you could ball."

JC snagged his rebound and returned to the free throw line, not bothering to look up. "Please don't ever say that again."

I stepped onto the court. Starting my day with Cliff and ending it with JC was the last thing I expected, but there I was, standing in the yellow hue that blanketed the cement with only ten minutes to go before the streetlights kicked on. "Do you hate me or do you *really* hate me?"

"That depends." He took another shot. "You bring a ball pump?"

"Do lips count?"

JC let the basketball roll off then met me near the bleachers. "Not exactly."

"Haven't seen you around much," I mumbled. "You been busy?"

"Busy ducking the cops swarming Jefferson." He ran his hand through his sandy brown curls then reached for a water bottle. "I heard BC wasn't Jacob's ex."

"Did you hear about Guy?" I asked.

JC nodded. I could tell something was wrong by the way he didn't react whatsoever.

"Look, I know you're mad at me . . ."

"Pissed." He scanned me up and down. "But I understand why you did it."

My eyes softened.

"It was fucked," he continued. "Like, seriously, *seriously* messed up. But you and Cliff were only trying to protect us."

I wiped the smile off my face. "You're the first one to say that."

"It doesn't make it okay."

"I know . . ."

"Nothing will ever make it okay," JC continued. "What we did that night, what we did to BC—" He paused and rolled his shoulders back. "Look, I don't want to talk about it."

"We don't have to."

"Ever again," he replied.

"Okay." I lifted my hands in surrender. "Never again."

JC dropped down on the bleachers and stared out across the court. The distant sound of children playing tickled my ears as I waited for him to replace it with words of his own. Eventually, he did. "Piper looked at me the whole time . . ."

I slowly turned my head.

"I, uh, I just told her to keep looking at me, not down at the body, and she did." His eyes lost themselves on the playground. "It was like she needed me again . . . I'd forgotten how much I missed that."

"I thought you didn't want to talk about it," I mumbled, realizing his love for his ex was just about as gone as mine was.

"Yeah." He sniffed and shook off the thought. "Yeah, I don't."

In a desperate attempt to change the subject, I brought up the next worse thing I could've. "Look, I'm sorry about the profile, JC. There was nothing I could do to stop him from shredding it."

"It's fine."

"No, it's not fine," I replied. "I wanted to help you."

"You did help me, Sonny. I mean, had it not been for you and all your crazy plans, I wouldn't be where I am today."

"Jefferson Sucks High?"

"Focused," he replied. "Focused on what truly matters." JC sighed. "You have a *really* weird way of showing it, and you might just be the most hypocritical person I've ever met, but you'd do anything for your friends . . . and I'll never forget what you've done for me."

My eyes swelled with tears. I'd never heard him say such nice things to me before, and call me pessimistic, but they almost seemed too nice.

"I'm going to lay low for a while," he continued, "put my energy into wrestling while it counts then book it the hell out of this town the first chance I get." JC dropped his head then rolled it toward me. "I'll be okay, Sonny. You will be, too."

"Are you—*are you breaking up with me*?"

"For now." He nodded. "I just need some time, you know? I need to forget about everything."

"Won't space just make you remember?"

"I don't know," he replied. "I guess we'll find out." I followed his every move while he stood to his feet and tossed his bag across his chest, tarrying on the asphalt as if he weren't sure of his decision. "Don't let that school take you down," he mumbled. "If anyone can survive Westcott High, it's you."

There *is* one thing worse than reaching the end of a chapter . . . and that's realizing you won't get to read the next one.

10 GLIMMER OF HOPE

How do you see a glimmer of hope amidst catastrophe? What would make you think it's there when you're surrounded and a return to life as you know it seems impossible?

I've always wondered if hope isn't so obvious. Maybe you can't always see it. Maybe you have to go find it.

"So how hard are we talking? Like, 'what was that tap?' hard or 'that might leave a mark' hard?"

"Winston, please," I replied. "You've seen me play dodgeball."

He slowly shook his head. "I never thought I'd see the day you and Kyle split ways."

"How 'bout the day when JC and I would?"

"He's just keeping his distance," Winston offered, his elbow bumping into my side.

“Speaking of distance, can you create some here? You’re right on top of me.”

“I’m not the only one.” His eyes scanned the faces of all the students suddenly pushing in close to us. “It looks like everyone is heading toward the cafeteria . . .”

In the distance, I saw Norah’s head bobbing up and down amongst the sea of students, her eyes on something behind me. “Kyle! Cliff! Come quick!” I followed her gaze, and my eyes landed at the other end of the hall where they stood—separately. “It’s Dean!”

“*Dean*?” I whipped around, jogging ahead of them through the crowd. They quickly passed me and turned into the common room. No thanks to Winston, we got there shortly after. I released his wrist and pushed my way through the huddle, struggling to get a glimpse of what everyone was staring at.

“Bro, what the hell are you doing?!” Kyle grabbed Dean’s fist before he could land another punch on his teammate’s face then pulled him to his feet.

“Trying to kill the guy?” Cliff asked, kneeling beside Lance, the victim of Dean’s wrath. Lance grabbed his bloody lip and peered at his captain as if the latter had betrayed him, and by the looks of it, he had.

“What happened?” Kyle shoved Dean in the chest.

Dean caught his balance, but barely. “He was talking shit.”

"We got into an argument about an offensive play," Lance fired back, taking Cliff's hand and wobbling to his feet. "You've lost your mind, Ballinger!"

Dean lurched toward his teammate, but Kyle held him back. "Go." He pointed toward the exit, giving Dean another shove. "I mean it, man, go!"

Dean grabbed his flushed cheek and spun around where he was greeted by dozens of scowls. He found me amongst those standing there, but he walked on, clearly unmoved by the fear in my eyes.

I couldn't understand the change in him. It was one thing to curse the day he ever met me after realizing I'd let Jacob into my life or resent me for what happened in the woods. It was another thing entirely to take his anger out on his point guard.

Realizing I'd lost eyes on Winston, I ventured back into the hallway to search for him.

"Déjà vu?"

My head rolled to the right, and I locked eyes with the last person on the planet I wanted to see. Suddenly, the crowded hall seemed empty, as if we were the only two people in it. "I'm sorry?"

"The fight," Guy replied. "Not too long ago, you guys were trying to fight me."

"Oh." I shook my head. "Yeah . . . right."

Guy opened his messenger bag and slipped a hand in, pausing for a second to look me over. "You okay, Sonny?"

"Why wouldn't I be?"

"You look a little clammy."

"I don't think you're supposed to say that to a girl," I replied, "or to anyone, for that matter."

"Wise words."

"I should get—"

"Here." He shoved a paper into my hand before I could finish my sentence. "Take one."

I lowered my head, and BC's smile flashed before me. "*Jesus*." I felt a jolt in my bones as I folded the flyer in half. "I, um—"

"Something wrong?"

"No, I just—" I glanced up. "I just wasn't expecting to see that."

"Nothing to be scared of, right?" He closed his bag. "That's my friend, Brystol. The one who's missing."

"Yeah . . . I think I saw her on the news."

"She's pretty, huh?"

"Very." I nodded. "Look, I should go check on my friends."

"Speaking of which . . ." Guy stared at the corner of the ceiling. "JC . . . I'm pretty sure he knows her."

"Her?"

"BC," he replied.

"I, um—" I scoured the halls for someone to save me. "I think they went to school together."

"Go."

"I'm sorry?"

"They *go* to school together," he corrected. "*Went* makes it sound like she won't be returning."

"Right." I kicked myself for the slipup. "Yeah, I'm sure she'll be returning any day now."

Guy's eyes narrowed. "You know what's funny? She, uh, she told me she met you at the Jefferson homecoming dance."

"Really?" I shrugged, searching his face as nonchalantly as I could to get a read on him. "Yeah, maybe."

"She said the two of you talked."

"I talked to a lot of people that night."

"Of course." He grinned. "She was the one with the huge crown on her head."

"Shouldn't you be delivering mail?" Cliff asked, joining us not a moment too soon.

Guy gave him a quick once-over before doing the same to me.

"Leave," Cliff demanded, and with that, he finally did.

When Guy was out of sight, I stared down at the blood on Cliff's hands. "Lance okay?"

"Your fucking psycho boyfriend isn't!"

"He's not my boyfriend."

“He’s losing it.” Cliff glanced over his shoulder. “Guy just watched him come unhinged the very same day he started handing out these posters. How do you think that looks?”

“I’ll talk to him.”

“Yeah, you better.”

“I said I will, alright?!” I pushed out a deep breath, watching my classmates walk by with BC’s blown-up face in their hands. “Did you schedule the meeting?”

Cliff nodded. “Tomorrow night. The football field.”

“The football—”

“Billy Poland!” Principal Clemmons appeared at the head of the hall in a notched lapel suit, bending a finger in the air like it was urgent. Before I could turn back around, Buckets was already passing us.

“What the hell?” Cliff whispered.

“Yeah,” I mumbled. “That.”

I watched Clemmons and Buckets exchange a few words before walking side by side toward the office.

“I’ll catch up with you later,” I said, starting to follow them there. Luckily, I ran into someone who could give me answers before I had to make the half-mile journey.

“Mr. Harrison?” He lifted his head from the water fountain and followed my gaze. “Do you know where he’s going?”

“Unfortunately, yes,” he sighed. “The hospital.”

As I rode the elevator to the third floor, the smell of disinfectant made me wish I'd gone home after school instead. I loathed any building that made me think of cleaning products, rubber, and warmed-up, three-day-old *pho*.

I struggled not to think of BC while being there, fought not to consider just how differently that night would have gone had my bumper not taken her out. Maybe I would have found myself in the hospital the days following instead of ankle-deep in dirt and sticks.

"Can I help you?"

I smiled at the medical receptionist as I approached the desk. Most of the walls were stark white, but the one behind her head was peach with three watercolor paintings of window planter boxes on top. "I'm here to see Buck—Billy. Billy Poland."

"Is he a patient?"

"No," I replied. "He, um, his—"

"Are you family?"

"I'm, um—"

"You're what?" she asked as if she already knew the answer. She seemed nice enough, but clearly didn't want to deal with one more person trying to bypass their policies. "You'll have to come back at five."

I pressed my lips together and nodded, swiveling on the polished floor. Had I made it to the elevator, I'm certain I would have burst into tears as soon as I stepped inside. Luckily for me, I was called back before I could.

"*Sonny*?"

"Why didn't you tell anyone?" I asked, leaving the vending machine behind in search of a table.

Buckets located one in the corner of the cafeteria and plopped down. "It never came up."

"How long has she had it?"

"Since Christmas," he answered, fighting to open his honeybun. "It's hard to fathom. She's only nine, you know?"

The pain in his eyes was fresh. The truth hadn't had time to settle into every inch of him—become him—and change who he was.

"But she's okay," he continued, and I wasn't sure who he was trying to convince. "Her, um, her ketones are high, but her DKA test came back negative."

"DKA?"

"Diabetic ketoacidosis."

I squirmed. "Buckets, I had no idea your little sister was diagnosed with this."

"Never came up," he repeated, his eyes losing focus as he stared at the tabletop. After discovering the timeline, I could see why. "Things have been crazy lately. Just never seemed like the right time to mention it."

"Yeah . . . about that . . ."

"We don't have to talk about it," he interjected.

"We should."

He shook his head while tearing into his snack.

"Buckets, you know I was only doing what I thought was best for all of us. I never meant to hurt you."

"It's fine."

"It's not fine," I replied. "It's so obviously not fine."

"Look, not to be blunt, Sonny, but Hannah is lying in a hospital bed right now. The last thing I want to do is discuss what happened that night." He lowered his honeybun then tossed it on the wrapper.

"Yeah." I tucked my chin. "Yeah, no, of course."

Silence joined us at the table, heavier than the words we were avoiding. I hadn't spoken to him since the woods, and like JC, it didn't appear as though he wanted to discuss much.

"I remember the day I passed the entrance exam," he mumbled, setting a new conversation in motion. "I was so excited to get tossed into the lottery, but I had my doubts I'd get picked. I haven't always been the luckiest guy in the world." A smile crept to his lips. "When we got the email, Hannah threw me this crappy little congratulatory party. She had my mom buy a sheet cake from the store and wrote Westcott High across the front in purple gel."

"Wrong color," I mumbled.

He huffed, and his smile petered out. “She was so happy I got in. I think she thought her big brother was going to be something great—do something great.”

“You *have*,” I whispered, placing my hand on his wrist. “Buckets, you’ve accomplished what some kids would give their right arm for—you’re here, and you’re going to make something of yourself.”

He dropped his head, but I pressed on.

“One day, when I’m standing on a busy New York street, I just *know* I’ll reach over for a fancy editorial magazine and see your name beneath the most beautiful photos. You’re going to get through this, okay? I know you feel terrible, we all do, but this will pass. It’s all going to pass.”

“Do you think she’d still look up to me,” he asked, “if she found out what I did?”

“Hannah isn’t going to find out,” I replied. “No one is. No one ever has to know.”

“But *I* know.” Buckets lifted his head, tears ready to fall. “I’ll always know, Sonny.”

My mouth hung open while his statement sunk in, and all I could do was lunge forward to embrace him. Our hug terrified and pained me all at once. Realizing how badly that night in the woods affected everyone sparked something within me.

The urge to protect my friends from any more pain grew far beyond what I thought possible. I had to make it all go away—to get things back to normal—and there, in a dismal cafeteria, I resolved that I would.

"Well, if it isn't my long-lost daughter."

"Hi, Mr. Ballinger."

"What a nice surprise!" With a book in one hand, he pulled the door back with the other, welcoming me inside his home before knowing I wasn't welcome. "Where've you been hiding?"

"In my books like you?"

His boisterous laugh filled the foyer as I stepped inside. "We always were the readers of the family, huh?"

"Proudly," I replied, forcing a smile.

"Try to rub off on Dean there, would ya?" He winked then poked his head toward the staircase. "Hey, Dean? Dean, you have company!"

"I'm sure he'll come down," I said, tucking my fingers into my back pockets. I felt strange standing there with him, knowing what my father put him through back on Baron Street all those months ago. The sporting goods store debacle was long buried, but the aftermath lived on.

Funny how that happens.

"Well, come in here, and talk to me." Mr. B started toward the kitchen, and with no other choice, I followed. "Can I get you something to drink?"

"No, thanks."

"Eat?"

"I'm good," I replied, my eyes landing on the full horror behind the living room wall. Clothes were strewn across the couches, piles of unopened mail were on every end table, and had it not been for the framed photo of Mrs. Ballinger hanging on the wall, I would've thought I was standing in the middle of a frat house.

"How's school been?" He grabbed a beer from the fridge, pushing a stack of bills to the side to clear a space on the counter.

"School's good."

"Raking in those A's?"

"Always," I managed to say, my eyes still dancing around the cluttered den.

"And what about Dean? How's he holding up?"

"Holding up?"

"You know, since, uh—"

"Since . . . ?"

"Ah." He took a swig from the bottle. "He didn't tell you."

"Tell me what?" I asked.

A loud thump from the backyard caught my attention. I jerked my head toward the sliding glass door just as the driveway lights shot on.

"I met someone," he said, and my eyes returned to the kitchen. Suddenly, fist-fighting the point guard made a lot more sense.

"It's still new." He spoke with excitement, cackling like a love-drunk teenager. "Only been a few months, but she's—" He paused. "Well, she's great."

"That's amazing," I mumbled.

"Sure is." He stared down at his beer, mindlessly picking at the paper while his smile faded. "Told Dean about it."

"And he's not as happy as you are?"

"No," he rasped. "No, he's not."

I glanced out the door, watching as Dean lugged two pieces of wood across the lawn.

"You know how much that boy loved his mom," he continued. "And I'm not trying to hurt Dean; I'm not. I just want to find a little happiness while I still can." I turned my head in time to watch him wipe his misty eye. He took another swig then lifted his bottle toward the living room. "And it wouldn't hurt to have a little help with the laundry around here."

We shared a smile in the dimly lit kitchen, plates stacked in the sink, two bottles of dish soap beside it. The time on the stainless-steel stove was wrong, and the dingy clock on the wall was ticking. Nothing made sense, but for the first time in weeks, everything did.

"I'll let you kids talk," he said, retiring to his bedroom.

I crossed the room and wrapped my fingers around the white handleset, slowly sliding the glass door open and revealing myself to Dean. His eyes shot to mine and never left.

"Taking up carpentry?"

Two sawhorses and a surfboard stood between us, its body scratched and pastel colors faded.

"Getting this ready to use for summer," he muttered, reaching for a sanding pad and breaking our gaze. His knuckles were raw and swollen, and I had a strong feeling it wasn't from the buffing.

I stepped into the grass and met him in the middle of the lawn. "Lance didn't rat you out, you know?" The sound of the sandpaper grinding against the board was almost unbearable, but I bit my tongue and dealt with it. "I don't know about his pride, but his face seemed to be okay."

Dean went on sanding, not bothering to look up or respond. His arm moved faster across the board.

"Hannah's in the hospital," I continued. "Buckets' sister, Hannah. I just came from there."

"Sorry to hear that," he mumbled, and I could tell that he was.

"Cops are all over Jefferson, by the way. JC told me. He said—"

"Look—why are you here?" Dean asked, jolting to an abrupt stop.

"I wanted to check on you—"

"I don't need you to check on me," he interrupted, tossing the pad into a nearby bucket and reaching for another. "I don't need to be filled in on anything, and I really don't need to see you."

I'm sure he expected me to leave, but I was done doing that. It's not what he needed. It's not what he *wanted.* I knew him well enough to know that.

I watched him get back to work on the board, waiting for the perfect amount of time to pass before I took another stab at him. "You know she can't replace your mom."

His sanding abruptly halted again. He kept his arms stretched and his head down, pausing for a moment before continuing.

"*Nobody* could," I added. "Remember that time we went with her to the produce stand out on Main? It was five thirty, and they closed at six, but she was determined to get those peaches come hell or high water. We jumped in her Suburban and went ninety all the way there, and, oh God, the clouds. Do you remember the clouds? They were point-two seconds away from exploding, but it's like she didn't even care. We sped into that gravel parking lot and stocked up on fruit with three minutes left." I laughed under my breath. "Naturally, it started pouring right around the time your mom misplaced her keys. The three of us ran around that market like crazy people looking for them, and she knocked down an entire stand of cantaloupes."

Dean continued sanding.

"She found her keys sitting in between two watermelons," I continued. "We rushed to the car, but by then it didn't matter. We were soaked and muddy, and she yelled at us for getting her car dirty, but we just laughed. When she realized how nuts she was being, so did she."

Dean's arm slowed.

"There will never be another Mrs. B," I said, staring down at his messy brown hair. "It would be silly to think otherwise."

His arm stopped.

"Look, if you want to hate me for what I did, then fine. If you never want to see me again after graduation, you'll never have to. If you want to resent your dad for trying to move on or blame the doctors for not being able to save your mom, then do it. Be mad at the world, Dean. Be mad at yourself. But for God's sake, don't stay that way."

I wasn't sure my speech swayed him as he stood there with nothing to say. He never replied or moved or gave me any indication that I'd made an impact.

Frustrated, I crossed my arms and shook my head, then swiveled in the grass and made my way toward the sliding glass door.

"It was strawberries."

I stopped in my tracks.

"She found her keys between two buckets of strawberries," he added. "Not watermelons."

I slowly turned around, and our eyes met. They stayed locked in until Dean broke our gaze and reached for a new pad.

A glimmer of hope isn't always so obvious. Sometimes, it's hidden just beyond those dark clouds overhead, and other times, if you look really closely, it's tucked inside a sentence about low-growing herbaceous plants with little green leaves.

11 CERTAINTY

I'm convinced of one thing: nobody wants to be certain. Certainty is scary. It leaves no room for chance or doubt, and doubting yourself is safe. You can claim you're going to climb that mountain, but if you doubt it, failure is easier to swallow when you inevitably fall short. Doubt is that security blanket that's not really warming you—that safety net that's not really saving you—but you choose it every time.

Because nobody wants to be certain of anything. Though you could always be right . . . you could always be wrong.

"Did you get one yet?"

Norah walked beside me into the science lab. Her soft pink shirt and fruity perfume were a step up from all the gray she'd been wearing, but she was far from being back to her normal self.

“Yesterday,” I replied, staring into BC’s deep brown eyes. I couldn’t believe it, but they were starting to haunt me more than Jacob’s.

“That freak is handing these posters out like candy on Halloween.” She tucked the paper into her book bag and followed me to my table. “When are you going to admit you’ve completely screwed us?”

“I’m assuming you’ve been filled in?” I dropped my bag and sighed. “Look, Guy doesn’t know anything, okay? He’s just trying to scare us.”

“You don’t know what he knows.”

“I know that he—”

“You don’t know shit,” she interjected, leaning over her folded arms. “It’s only a matter of time before Guy points the police in our direction. You didn’t save us from an investigation, Sonny. You started a new one.”

“I’m handling it, okay?”

The classroom was filling up, and she noticed. “Make it quick,” she said, glancing over both shoulders. “One more poster, and I lose my shit.”

“Calm down.”

“Do *not* tell me to calm down!” She leaned in, and her fruity fragrance smacked me in the face. I suppose it was better than if she had. “I don’t want to come to school every morning and see the girl we buried in the woods taped to my locker!”

"And you think I do?!"

"Then make it stop," she demanded. "Make it all stop."

"Everyone listen up for their names!" yelled my science teacher, starting class not a moment too soon.

Norah turned on the ball of her foot like a jewelry box ballerina on its last crank then started toward her table.

If I was still thankful for just one thing after our heated exchange, Westcott High's policy to use synthetic animals for dissection instead of real ones topped the list. I pushed my forceps and scalpel to the side, making room for whomever was about to be called.

Unfortunately, the partner Mr. Broom assigned to me was anything but happy about it.

"Uh—" Jacob lifted his finger in the air. "Can we switch?"

"I was just hoping someone would ask that," he replied. "Absolutely not."

Jacob pushed out a deep breath and slowly rolled off his stool. I almost felt like I owed him an apology for existing given the way he dragged his feet in my direction.

"I guess you're my partner?"

"Guess so," he replied, reaching for the tweezers.

For the next fifteen minutes, Jacob's eyes went from the worksheet to the cat and never once landed on me. Mine, however, managed to scour every inch of him. His faded navy-blue hoodie and ripped, dark blue jeans bounced off his clean white sneakers. His once tanned skin coming off a

California summer had turned to a lighter olive shade. And his silence was driving me absolutely mad.

"Are you really just going to sit there and ignore me?" I asked, slapping my scalpel against the table.

Jacob made an incision straight across the feline's stomach. "There's nothing to talk about."

"I think there's plenty to talk about."

"There's not."

"Jacob, please," I reasoned, the only thing between us a bitter mood I couldn't dispel. "How can you tell me you love me, tell me you'll wait, then turn around weeks later and kick me out of your house?"

"Don't do that." He looked up for the first time in nearly twenty minutes. "Don't take what I said to you and throw it in my face."

"I'm not!"

"Please work silently," commanded Mr. Broom, peering at us over the top of his glasses.

I sighed, allowing another minute to pass before pressing on. "Look, I know I've been a little confusing lately—"

Jacob huffed.

"*I know* I've been distant," I continued. "And as much as I'd love to sit here and explain things to you, I can't."

"Why not?"

"Because I don't even understand everything myself!"

“I think you do,” he argued. “I think you know exactly why you’ve been distant.”

“This has nothing to do with—”

“Then tell me what’s going on,” he replied. “If it’s not Dean, tell me what else has your attention.”

With so many uncertainties hanging in the balance, how could I tell him the truth? I still didn’t know how BC knew him, why she pretended to be his ex, or how he’d react to finding out I was behind those missing person posters. Telling him what had my attention wasn’t an option. The only one I had left was allowing him to believe what he already did.

“Yeah.” Jacob nodded. “Thought so.”

“Jacob—”

“I’m taking Alice Kennedy to Reels next weekend,” he interjected, standing to his feet.

The end of January was quickly approaching, which was only important if one was interested in attending Westcott’s annual drive-in movie festival. Under nothing but the moon and string lights, lovebirds could enjoy a motion picture while curled up in a plaid blanket, sipping cider.

It sounded just as romantic as it was.

Assuming I misunderstood, I narrowed my eyes and waited for a follow-up statement.

“She asked me to go with her,” he offered, gathering his belongings. Still, I was unable to comprehend what he was saying.

"What—what are you even—"

"Just thought you should hear that from me." Jacob stepped beside our table, stopping to take a good look at me before walking back to his.

I rolled my head in his direction, catching the tail end of a curious stare from Alice, who flipped a mint-julep-and-jade-striped paper in her notebook before turning back to her work.

"You're early!"

"You're late," Cliff called, standing tall on the turf.

I checked my wristwatch as I made the long walk toward him. "I'm right on time."

"If you're not early, you're late," he deadpanned, side-eying me as I took my position. We stood side by side, facing the entrance to the field while impatiently waiting for Casey to arrive.

"Where's your sling?"

"Took it off."

"Yeah, I can see that," I quipped. "Why?"

"Talk to Dean?" he asked.

My eyes narrowed. "Yes, I talked to Dean."

"And?"

"And I'm thinking you should talk to Norah."

He raised an eyebrow. "Why's that?"

"Because if you think Dean's losing his mind, she's definitely lost hers."

Cliff tucked his hands into his hoodie pockets, looking at everything but me. "What'd she say?"

"Something along the lines of 'one more poster and I rage.'" I glanced at him, trying to gauge what he was thinking. "She's completely freaking out about Guy Penn."

"He's a troubled kid," Cliff mumbled. "Rich grandparents, pull with Winchester, but he got into dozens of fights at his old school. I don't know how seriously the police will take him if he brings them our names."

"So what are you saying?"

"I'm saying he'll need more than his suspicions to get something moving."

"Okay? Like what?"

"Corroboration," he replied. "He'll need someone else to validate them."

I took a second to scan the dreary field, ensuring no one else was there though I knew we were alone. "I don't understand," I whispered. "Who's going to do that?"

"I don't know . . ." Cliff rolled his shoulders back and widened his stance, lifting his chin at the sound of a car door slamming. "But I can tell you who's not."

Maybe being certain isn't such a bad idea. Though things will probably turn out right . . . they could always turn out wrong.

12 UNEXPECTED GUESTS

Unexpected guests seldom meet a welcome. At least, that's what my mother used to tell me when Grandma and Grandpa Carter would pop in to say hello. "A little notice goes a long way," she'd say. Mostly because that notice gives you time to shove your dirty laundry in the garage until they leave.

But there are some guests who don't need to announce they're stopping by. And by the end of that day, I was going to have one.

Freshman Year

"That's enough!" Kyle jerked his head to the left, but my paintbrush followed him.

"If you don't let me finish the three, it's going to look like you have a P on your cheek," I snapped back.

"For pretty boy," mumbled an Archwick senior as a herd of green letterman jackets trekked toward their changing room. The Crescent College Showcase, or CCS, was held at a college campus in Nevada, and it wasn't nearly large enough to hold all the egos traveling here.

Kyle grabbed my paintbrush and completed the number, using his cell-phone screen as a mirror. "There. Thirteen. Happy?"

"I would've been much happier doing it myself!"

"Yeah, well, you're not even supposed to be here, let alone using face paint." Kyle smacked my hand away before it reached his cheek.

"For your information, my dad was very happy to have a flying buddy." I dug through my bag and removed our itinerary. "Besides, if I hadn't come, who would've kept him on schedule?"

"When our chaperone needs a chaperone, we're in trouble." Kyle dropped his heavy bag and peered out the double glass doors. "What's taking everyone so long to leave the hotel? We need to warm up before the showcase starts."

"You're early," I replied.

"If you're not early, you're late." He let out a deep breath, forcing smiles at important men in collared shirts.

"And you're nervous . . ."

"No!"

"It's written all over your face," I argued.

"How could you possibly see that over the stupid paint?" Kyle swiveled around and dunked his cheek into a nearby water fountain. "Get this off of me, please."

I followed him, retrieving a napkin from my bag. "Take it easy, Ky."

"I'm—I'm fine."

"It's okay if you aren't. This is a big deal. Qualifying for the showcase—and as a freshman?"

"I just want to play well."

"You will." I dried his face. "You and Cliff together are this weird, unstoppable, weird, crazy-talented duo."

"Hey, do you think we're weird?" He lifted his eyes to the double doors and smiled. "Look what the cat dragged in."

"Yo," Cliff replied, strolling inside shoulder to shoulder with Mr. Reynolds. The two were a particularly intimidating pair. "The other guys here yet?"

"A few. We were waiting for you."

"I wasn't," I mumbled under my breath before greeting the new arrival. "Hi, Mr. Reynolds."

The man didn't seem to be able to hear me over his anticipation. "Son, I'm going to find Coach T. See you out there."

"Yeah."

"Play smart," he warned, patting his son's arm before stalking off.

“Yeah.” Cliff widened his eyes and dragged them toward Kyle. “You ready?”

“I think so . . .”

“We’ve done these drills a hundred times,” he replied. “You can do them in your sleep.”

“I’m just—”

“He’s nervous,” I interjected.

Cliff nodded, studied him, then extended his fist. “One team.”

Kyle rolled his eyes but managed to crack a grin.

“Come on, man, say it.”

“Here?”

“Anywhere and everywhere,” Cliff replied.

He bumped fists—it was a small gesture, but I knew that, to Kyle, it meant the end of his butterflies. “Twenty brothers,” he mumbled as the doors behind us flung open.

In walked a wide-eyed ninth grader with a mean throwing arm and an even meaner face.

“There’s that Sawyer kid,” Kyle whispered. “The quarterback at Bella View.”

Cliff eyed him as he strolled by with a few brothers of his own. Their royal-blue jackets weren’t easy on the eyes, but if I were being totally honest, they were. “Let’s go,” he stammered, starting toward Westcott’s dressing room. “Coach T is probably looking for us.”

As quick as a magnet, Kyle followed, but he glanced back at me before they got too far. "Sit in the stands, okay?"

"Okay!" I hollered, shuffling my feet with nowhere to go. "I'll be watching!"

"Watch your feet."

A red-haired beauty joined me on the bleachers not too long after I'd started to get excited for some quiet. Her locks were long and wild, and her jeans were ripped and loose. She plopped down beside me and tore into a bag of candy. "Alice."

"Sonny." I scooted down a tad. "Are you from—"

"Bella View. My brother's number twenty-two; Dad's the coach."

"Cool."

"You're a Westcotter?" Her smirk told me she already knew. "I think our principal's son goes there."

"Kyle." I nodded. "He's my best friend."

"I guess his parents split?"

"That's one way to put it," I replied, lifting my chin toward the field. "He's number thirteen."

"Cute," she gawked. "Freshman?"

I nodded.

"Same. Liam's a senior, and he never lets me forget it when I talk about boys."

"Protective?"

"That's one way to put it," she replied, tossing a sour worm into her mouth. "So what's it like over at Westcott?"

"Uh—strict?"

She laughed freely, like the cruel world hadn't happened to her yet. "The other day, my English teacher made me spit my mint out before I took my test. She said it might distract me. A *mint*?!"

I smiled, semi-acquainted with said world. "That sounds pretty intense."

"It was." Alice adopted a British accent and waved her hands through the air. "I mean, is a mint-chewing test-taker not Ivy League approved? We simply can't do anything that would jeopardize a full ride, now can we?"

"Why do I get the feeling the only crescent you want anything to do with is the roll you can eat?"

She shrugged. "It's just not my thing, you know? The competition, the rivalry. I'd much rather be at a normal school."

"What's a normal school?" I asked.

"One where freshening your breath isn't seen as a crime." Alice dropped her head. "Liam says it's going to change me . . ."

"Bella View?"

She raised a brow then nodded once. "Into a punctual, proper, prissy little princess."

"That's a lot of P's."

"Like, a ton," she replied. "I told him he was crazy, but he sounded pretty sure of it."

After an hour of witty conversation with the likable tomboy, I swung my knees toward hers. "Why don't we make a pact?"

"A pact?" she questioned. "I don't know . . . I don't think I'm supposed to like you . . ."

"Well, I like you."

Alice squinted and gave it some thought. "Yeah." She scrunched her nose. "I like you, too. Let's do it."

"A promise"—I grabbed her pale hands and squeezed—"that we will *always* stay the same."

She reached into her bag and pulled out two worms—not as strong as a blood oath, but it worked. "The exact same."

I downed the gummy and we shared a smile, but hers quickly petered out while she stared across the field. "It probably won't though, you know? *Change me*." She waved at her dad with dead eyes, slowly swallowing. "I mean, how could it, right? It's just a school."

"There's my number P!" I pulled Kyle in for a sweaty hug following the four-hour-long camp. "You did so good!"

"Thanks," he replied, chugging a sports drink. "Did you see Cliff? He was on his A game."

"*You* did amazing," I said. "And listen, if we leave now, you'll have time to shower before we hit that candy apple shop right down the street from the hotel. They close in an hour."

"Actually, the, uh, the guys were going to go out for pizza . . ."

"Oh." I tucked my hands into my back pockets and looked at everything but him. "Oh, yeah, of course. You should go."

Kyle paused then pressed his lips together and tapped my upper arm. "Let me go say bye to Cliff."

My eyes whispered *thank you*, and I waited patiently in the hallway for him to return. Conversations between coaches trickled through the air, and one by one, players from every end of the Crescent rolled out of their dressing rooms. For ten minutes, none of them were Kyle.

Fearing I'd miss my chance at a Nevada-famous candy apple, I followed the smell of sweat and body spray until I reached the source—a room with *Westcott High* taped across the front, and a Royal Blue from Bella View pressing his ear to the crack of the door.

Through the walls, I could hear Cliff and Kyle arguing, and Kyle sounded frantic. I couldn't make out much, but from what I could tell, he'd eavesdropped on the wrong conversation—and heard something he wasn't supposed to.

"What are you doing?"

Sawyer jumped then swiveled around with an expression I'll never forget. His nostrils flared, and his eyes were wide, his gaze on fire. He looked as shocked as he was angry—and boy, was he angry.

Kyle and Cliff fled to the hallway.

"You can't be serious," Sawyer spat, immediately digging his claws in. "You're an OC?"

"OC?" I squinted. "What's that?"

"An Odds Compiler," he replied. "Your fucking friend here works for a bookie."

"Listen, man, take it easy," Kyle urged.

"You telling people what I'm worth, Reynolds? You putting a price tag on Bella View?" Sawyer sized Cliff up, but I still wasn't sure who had the advantage. "How much money you make off this showcase, huh?"

"It's just a few stupid guys placing bets, alright?"

"It's a gambling ring, Winchester, and it's illegal. It sure as hell breaks the SCC."

I glanced at Cliff, and I'd never seen him look so caught before. His eyes were void of emotion, and he sat back while Kyle fought his fight for him.

"Do you realize what you're doing?" Sawyer asked. "You'll be kicked out of the Crescent if they find out."

"Son? You back here?" Mr. Ellington shouted from the head of the hall.

"Please don't say anything," Kyle begged. "It'll stop."

"We promise," I added.

"Oh, you promise?" He tossed a high chin at Cliff. "What about you?"

But Cliff didn't respond. Maybe he didn't want to make a promise he didn't intend to keep.

"You have my word." Kyle took another stab at him. "It won't happen again."

Sawyer readjusted his gym bag, giving Cliff one last glare before heading back to Arizona.

Present Day

One hundred and twenty yards of turf sat beneath us. Three students, three different walks of life, all there for the very same reason—I just wish I knew what that reason was.

"I want to make a deal," Cliff stated, standing taut at the fifty-yard line.

Sawyer smirked, almost like he'd figured. "And what deal would that be?"

My breathing quickened at the sight of him. I was expecting Casey to arrive in a crew neck sweater with humility. I never anticipated seeing that snake from Bella View slither across the green.

"Casey told you something."

He shrugged. "Casey tells me a lot of things."

"This thing had to do with me."

I glanced at Cliff, and I didn't like the direction his tone had headed, almost like he was slinking toward defeat.

"Ah." Sawyer snapped his fingers then flashed his pearly whites. "The blackmail thing, yeah?"

Cliff clenched his jaw.

"Must've done something pretty bad," he continued. "She wouldn't give me any details."

"And you're not going to ask for them."

"Is that right?" Sawyer sized him up. "Pretty confident for a guy looking for a deal."

"I know what you did to Kyle. The position you put him in? Trying to convince him to turn on me?"

"Didn't work."

"Yeah, that'll never work," Cliff replied. He took a step forward, standing nose to nose with his nemesis. "Does your girlfriend know you tried using her as leverage?"

Sawyer grinned. "Let me guess . . . you're gonna tell her?"

"I'm not that petty."

"What are you then?"

"Injured." Cliff sounded as disappointed as he was furious. "I tweaked my shoulder. I'll tell Coach, and I'll extend my injury through summer workouts. In return? You won't poke Casey for information."

"Cliff?" I tugged on his arm, his offer much too large for a star quarterback on the fast track to Cornell.

"Do we have a deal?" he asked, cutting me off.

Sawyer hesitated, studying him with piercing scrutiny. I could tell he wasn't expecting to see Cliff nursing his arm, but maybe what he really saw was an opportunity. "Full bench?"

"Guaranteeing your play time in the first couple of games," he answered. "No more showcase bullshit, no more threats, and whatever the hell is going on between you and Langdon, do it at your own damn house."

"You expect me to just forget what I heard that day?"

"I expect you to realize you can't prove it."

Sawyer covered his laugh with a cupped hand. "What's your plan, Cliff? To keep stacking money until you get caught?"

"Don't worry about me."

"You were supposed to stop."

"I said don't worry about me." Cliff tightened his mouth and extended a hand forward. "You wanted my spot, right? Take it."

"Why don't you take some advice and stop acting like you know every damn thing? What you're doing is—"

"Why don't you stop acting like you give a *shit* about what I'm doing?" Cliff closed the tiny gap between them. "Take the deal."

One hundred and twenty yards, three students, two egos, one handshake . . . the recipe for a good old Westcott contract.

I suppose I'd witnessed stranger things.

Sawyer reached forward and squeezed Cliff's hand—but not harder than Cliff squeezed his, almost as if his body reacted to the bad agreement he was making.

"Don't make me regret this," Cliff mumbled, lending the torch.

Sawyer peeled his eyes off Cliff, glanced at me, then walked off the field with his new role as head quarterback. When he reached his car, I whipped around in a fury.

"Are you out of your mind?! Why would you do that?!"

"I didn't have a choice."

"The entire summer?!"

"*I didn't have a choice*," Cliff repeated, starting toward the parking lot. "He was going to get Casey to talk."

"She wouldn't have!"

"Really? Because it took her all of two seconds to tell him I blackmailed her."

I sighed, chasing him across the sod. "We were supposed to talk to her!"

"Yeah, well, now we don't have to."

"Cliff! I can't believe—"

"It's done," he replied, coming to a halt. He stared at me—through me—and warned me to shut up.

If only that had worked. "When are *you* going to be done? I don't care for the guy, Cliff, but he's right. What you're doing is stupid."

"Stay out of it."

"You don't even need the money!"

Cliff walked on.

"I don't understand why you'd risk your future to make a little cash."

"A little."

"A lot." I shrugged. "A ton. Look, I don't care how much you make, it's not worth it!"

"It's not your problem."

"Cliff—"

"God, would you just *fucking stop*?!" He whipped around, his eyes a little wetter. "Stop trying to psychoanalyze me. Stop trying to understand me."

"I'm—"

"You have no idea why I do what I do." His brows furrowed, like he couldn't believe he was arguing with scum like me. "You have no idea what I need."

"Cliff—"

"You don't know what I deserve, who I deserve—"

"Cliff, listen—"

"No, you listen!" he spat, veins bulging. "You *don't* know me, Sonny. Stop trying to."

His eyes told a thousand stories, none of which I understood.

Maybe that was a good thing.

"Alright," I mumbled, swallowing my concern. "Alright, I'll back off."

Cliff took a moment to survey me, a very long moment. "I need you to do something," he said, rolling his head toward the parking lot.

I tried moving on, but truthfully, I was still stuck on the thirty-yard line.

"Buckets—your friend—I need you to ask him for a favor."

"What kind of favor?"

Cliff kept walking toward his car, so I followed. "We need to get into Harriet Lange."

"The facility?"

"The system," he replied. "Buckets is into that shit, right?"

"I—I wouldn't exactly word it that way," I answered. "Why do we need in?"

"To see if BC was a patient there. If she was, her file might tell us some things we need to know."

"Like what?"

"Friends' names. People who could possibly corroborate Guy's suspicions."

"I don't know, Cliff. Buckets is going through some things right now. I'm not sure he'll be up for it."

"Things?"

"Family things," I replied. "His sister, Hannah . . . she was recently diagnosed with—" I paused, deciding to keep the news my own. "Look, I think Buckets is just trying to lay low."

Cliff huffed, clearly unable to relate.

"He's not in the same position we are, alright? He can't always take the same risks we can."

"So I'll pay him."

"Pay him? You can't just throw money at things, Cliff. That's not how it works."

"That's exactly how it works," he replied, yanking open his door and placing one leg inside his car. "Tomorrow night, my house—set the price."

"Happy Birthday!"

Casey peeked over her locker door to find my pathetic attempt at a tornado-shaped cupcake.

"I promise it's edible," I said as she removed it from my fingers, leaving between us still the Long Wall of Quảng Ngãi.

"I'll take your word for it . . ."

"New bracelet?" I asked, gawking at the thin, rose gold chain around her wrist.

Casey gave it a glance. "Gift from Sawyer."

"*Wow.*"

"Sweet, right?"

"Very." I slid my hands in my pockets and smiled disingenuously. "Kind of makes my cupcake look like trash."

Unamused, she flung her book bag over a shoulder and slammed her locker door. "I should get to first."

"Yeah," I replied, blinking at how quickly she shut me down. "Yeah, of course."

"But thanks for this." She lifted the glob of dark gray icing into the air as if to toast me.

I forced a smile before she turned then collapsed as soon as she did. My shoulders slumped while I watched her drift off, and I couldn't help but feel that things between us were beyond repair. It was hard to believe how much had changed in her life—or how much her role had changed in mine.

"Sonny?"

I blinked myself back to find Casey had come to a halt. "Ms. Winchester is taking us out for dinner tonight. Nothing special—just my brothers, Winston, and Kyle—but you should come."

"Tonight?" I asked, half-excited, half-remembering I'd arranged that meeting with Buckets.

"If you can't, it's fine."

"No, no, I can," I shouted, a real smile breaking free. "I'll, um, I'll be there."

"Would you look at you!"

My eyes shot to the right of my mirror, a dragon-red lipstick hovering near my mouth. "Hi, Dad."

"You always did know how to pick a dress," he mumbled.

"Yeah, well, this one kind of picked me." I popped my lips. "You like it?"

"Love it." He strolled across my carpet, plopping down on the edge of my bed. "Red has always been your color."

I looked down at the split side backless cami slip-on, running my fingers over the silk and desperately trying to push a crowned BC to the back of my mind. "Thanks for letting me stay here while Mom is out of town."

"That almost sounds like you had a choice," he joked. "So what's this dinner?"

"Just a birthday thing for Casey."

"Birthday thing, huh?"

"Yep," I replied, walking into my closet to retrieve a pair of strappy nude heels.

"Dean going?"

I rolled my eyes from behind the door. "Why would Dean be going?"

"Just a question . . ."

"I told you, Dad, Dean and I broke up."

"Oh, I know," he replied. "Just figured you'd work things out, that's all."

"Well, we've tried."

"Hard?"

"Hard!" I shouted, bent over, and struggling to fasten the buckle.

"Alright, alright." He let out a deep breath. "I just never did understand what happened between the two of you."

His statement made me pause. With crossed arms and enough resentment to fill the closet, I stalked back toward my bedroom, pausing beneath the door frame. I had been gone for so long, it almost looked like he was surprised to see me. "*You* did, Dad." His dark eyes met mine. "The stolen money. The setup. Mr. Ballinger, the fight, the fallout—"

"Sonny—"

"He dumped me," I continued, "because *you* happened. How could you not see that?"

Dad dropped his head and swallowed. "Well, I'm—I'm sorry to hear that, kid. I didn't know—"

"How could you have?" I shrugged. "You'd have to talk to me to know what's going on in my life."

"Now, that's not fair . . ."

"Oh, it isn't?"

"It's not like I haven't tried, Sonny."

"Unless your definition of 'trying' is spending all your free time with the wrestlers and completely checking out once you lost your coaching job, then I really don't think you have."

"You know I'm here for you girls." He stood to his feet and extended his palm toward the hallway. "We just had a fantastic Christmas together."

"Fantastic how?!"

"I got you every damn thing you wanted under the tree!"

"Is that supposed to mean something?" I treaded toward my vanity. "You ruined the only good thing I had."

"*Ballinger*?"

"Yes, Ballinger."

"*He* was the only good thing you had?"

"Nice." I grabbed my clutch and stomped off toward the door, but he stopped me, wrapping his large hands around my shoulders. I'd be lying if I said I wasn't glad. Had he let me leave my room, it likely would've been the last nail in our coffin.

"Look . . ." He sighed. "Look, I'm sorry, alright? I know you loved the boy. What happened between his father and me was rough on you both, and I get that, but I don't want it to ruin our relationship."

"You don't?"

"No, of course, I don't."

"Then tell me the truth," I demanded.

"The truth? What truth?"

"Why'd you take that money?"

Dad slowly released my shoulders, tilting his head at my weighted question. "Sonny . . ."

"*Why*, Dad?" I pleaded, desperate for his honesty. "Why'd you do it?"

Our staring contest came to an end when the doorbell rang, and Dad took that as his opportunity to avoid answering me. "You should go," he said. "You don't want to be late."

I wished he weren't right. I gave my clutch a squeeze and stepped around him, hoping he saw me shake my head at him along the way. Eager to greet Winston and leave, I rushed down the stairs and yanked the front door open. Unfortunately, my chauffeur for the evening wasn't standing there.

Unfortunately, someone else was. "I have a proposition for you."

Some guests don't need to inform you that they plan to visit . . . like the ones who already know they aren't welcome and don't exactly care.

13 THE TRUTH

When I was younger, proving I was an honest person seemed more important than knowing I was. Campaigning for my innocence when someone spread a lie about me felt like the most important job I could ever have. I was standing for something, someone: myself.

But as I grew up, I understood that fighting for the truth was a battle I couldn't win. Because no matter how honest a person you are, no matter how black-and-white it seems, there will *always* be people who won't believe it.

I fought a rising panic as I stared into Guy's eyes. Almost on cue, the front porch light burnt out, and nothing but the ashen sky behind him lit the scene.

"What are you doing here?" I asked, swallowing in an ill-fated attempt to conceal my fear.

Guy pulled his camel-colored beanie off his head, exposing his thick brown curls. "I'd like for you to attend Reels with me next weekend."

"*Reels*?"

"The drive-in movie festival," he said with a smile. "Thought it could be a fun time."

"Why—" I stepped outside, gently pulling the door along with me. "Why would you think that?"

Guy shrugged. "Doesn't it sound exciting? Big screen . . . under the stars . . . hot cider in matching mugs?"

"That sounds like a date . . ."

"Not my intention." He lifted his hands as if he were apologizing. "Just thought we could hang out, that's all."

"And, um—" I slipped my hand into my clutch and removed my cell phone, quickly canceling my ride with Winston by responding to his latest text. "And why would you want to do that?"

"To reconcile," Guy answered, eying my every move. "I think you and I got off on the wrong foot."

"You *think*?"

He grinned, took a step back, and placed his hand over his heart. "What do you say I make it up to you?"

Before I could decline, the front door swung open, and my dad joined us on the porch. "Is that Guy Penn?"

"Coach."

"What are you doing here?" he asked, leaning in for a hug.

"Dad, not now."

"You aren't here to wrestle, are you? I'll have my mat pulled out before you can blink."

"Uh, no, sir," he answered with a laugh. "Just trying to convince your daughter to attend Reels with me next weekend."

"Oh." Dad's eyes widened as much as mine. "I—I didn't know the two of you were—"

"We're not," I interjected, holding Guy's gaze. "Dad, could you give us a minute?"

"Sure . . ." He patted his former wrestler on the shoulder. "Good seeing you."

"You, too, sir. Hope to see you again soon."

"Stop by anytime," he replied, drifting toward the door.

Once it closed, I stepped forward with a question of my own. "What do you think you're doing?!"

"What do you mean?"

"You know what I mean," I hissed. "Why are you here at my house? Why are you pretending you want anything to do with me?"

"Pretending?"

I clenched my jaw, realizing I'd have to switch it up. "What do you want, Guy?"

"I told you." He shrugged. "I'd like for you to attend—"

"*What do you want*?" I tried again, refusing to accept his load of crap.

Guy stared deeply into my eyes and eventually broke. “To talk.”

His confession made me take a step back even though I knew it was coming. “Talk . . .” I swallowed. “Talk about what?”

“I don’t know,” he answered, reaching forward to remove a piece of string off my dress. His touch repulsed me, but I was far too nervous to fight it. “Stuff?”

My eyes followed his fingers as he flicked the string to the side, then they shot up to his. “You and I have nothing to discuss.”

“Nothing?”

“*No*.” With a red lip and no confidence, I stepped around him in pursuit of my car. “And there’s absolutely no reason why I’d agree to go *anywhere* with you.”

I considered what I must have looked like gawking through the window of the Italian restaurant. Maybe the guests assumed I’d just caught my boyfriend dining with another girl or that the corner table, far right, brought back the memories I made there with a lost loved one.

I lifted my hand to the glass door.

Perhaps the hostess assumed I was waiting for someone. The waiter taking the order at the table in front of me could have thought I was checking him out. But the truth?

The truth was I had other things to worry about—more pressing things—and though I knew it was wrong, I couldn't choose Casey.

"Nice dress."

"Long story," I mumbled, stepping inside Cliff's home. I unbuckled my heels as he closed the door.

"Need to talk about it?"

"No."

"Want some sweats?"

I considered his offer when I saw how comfortable he looked in his but declined. "We need to talk."

"Okay . . ." Cliff started toward the kitchen, and I followed. Up ahead, I saw a stack of money sitting on the island, but I didn't see Buckets until we walked into the room.

For a split second, I froze. "Hey?"

"What's up?" he asked, fidgeting on a nearby chair. I could tell he'd never been inside a house so nice, and he looked anything but comfortable.

"I, um, I didn't see your car . . ."

He took a swig of water then set his glass down on the kitchen table. "My mom—she's, uh—she's just thinking about selling it."

"Oh." My eyes shot to Cliff before I offered Buckets a smile. "I didn't know that."

“She dropped me off,” he continued. “Maybe you could drive me home?”

“Of course.” I nodded, deciding my news about Guy Penn wasn’t worth sharing—not with him, anyway. “Should we, um, should we get to work?”

Cliff widened his eyes and leaned over the counter as Buckets brought his laptop toward us.

“I can’t promise anything,” he said, setting up camp. “I’ll have to probe for weaknesses without triggering any alarms.”

“Do you think you’ll be able to get in?”

“I’m going to try.”

For the next two hours, we sat in agony while we waited for Buckets to gain access. Cliff and I had moved to the living room, and I rested on his unforgiving leather sectional using my fingers to iron out wrinkles that weren’t in my dress. He sat at the other end, his elbows in his knees, his face in his hands. The house was quiet—too quiet—and we were beginning to lose hope.

“Guys?” My eyes whipped to the open kitchen to see Buckets grinning at the screen. “I’m in.”

“No shit.” Cliff bolted for the island and hovered over his shoulder. My reaction was a bit different. The thought of being minutes away from knowing the truth about BC scared me more than I thought it would.

“You’re in?” I mumbled, pushing myself off the couch.

"Brystol, right?" Buckets' fingers got back to work. "Brystol Montgomery?"

"Is she in there?" Cliff asked.

The sound of keys tapping filled the kitchen as I strolled into the room, taking my place on the other side of Buckets.

"Brystol Montgomery," he mumbled like he couldn't believe he'd found her. "She's here."

"Can you pull her file?"

"It's downloading," he replied. "Three minutes."

Before we knew it, a plethora of psychotherapy notes popped up before our eyes—each one dated, each one signed.

"Scroll down to the first," Cliff ordered, waiting for the screen to stop. "June . . ."

"She was admitted at the start of summer," Buckets muttered.

"Maybe sending her there was the reason for their move," I suggested. "She said she came here for a fresh start. Maybe this was part of that."

"Click the note."

Buckets followed Cliff's lead, double-tapping the first entry in BC's patient portal. "This one's pretty generic . . ."

"Go to the next one," he replied.

"'Ms. Montgomery seemed to have an adequate response to treatment. Symptoms of low self-worth continue to be described. Her symptoms have remained the same . . .'"

"Next."

"'Ms. Montgomery denies suicidal thoughts or intentions. No sleeping problems reported . . .'"

"Click another one," Cliff demanded, getting into the investigation. "Any mention of family? Friends?"

Buckets skimmed through the next note. "Nothing."

"What's this?" I asked, pointing toward the bottom of the page. "'The patient expressed sadness over leaving her previous place of employment. Ms. Montgomery shared the following details during this session: "I miss my coworkers at Butterfly Café. I wish I never had to leave them."'"

"Butterfly Café?" Buckets pulled out his cell phone and typed in the name. "There's one not too far from here."

My mind raced as I watched him scroll through the photos online. The beautiful two-story glass building appeared to have a diner on the bottom and a butterfly house on top. "What's on that napkin?"

He clicked the picture and zoomed in. "Did you know butterflies actually have four wings, not two?"

"A quote?" Cliff asked.

"Butterfly facts," Buckets replied. "This one's cool: Small things can have non-linear impacts on complex systems."

"That's the butterfly effect," I whispered. "Where did you say this place is located?"

"I didn't." He scrolled back to the previous page. "Uh . . . Long Beach."

Suddenly, Cliff wasn't the most eager one in the room. "Go to the next note."

"Okay . . ." Buckets pulled up another entry. "'Patient expresses feelings of inadequacy. Denies suicidal thoughts or intentions . . .'"

"Next one."

"'Ms. Montgomery appeared calm and communicative in today's session. Symptoms of low self-worth continue to be described. Her symptoms, as previously reported, are unchanged.'"

"Keep going."

Buckets looked over at me then pulled up the next note. There, on entry seven, were the encrypted words I was searching for.

"'In today's session, the patient discussed her months-long infatuation with a gentleman who frequented Butterfly Café with his girlfriend. She described feeling anxious and wanted to refer to the customer as "him/he."'"

"*Him*?"

"Jacob . . ." Terror mounted with every word I read. "'Ms. Montgomery shared the following pertinent details during this session: "It was like they shared a love for food, and his face lit up when she'd bite into hers. I'd never seen anything like it, the care he showed her, the attention he gave her. She was his to protect. I've never felt protected before."'"

Buckets clicked the next note and highlighted the Content of Therapy log then read more of BC's admissions. """"She was pretty, and he liked that about her. He liked when she smiled. He liked her straight teeth. He liked her plump lips.""""

""""When he leaned over their table to kiss her, I imagined what that must have felt like. I wondered if she knew how lucky she was."""" I started to sweat as I read on. """"She was everything I wasn't—already a butterfly while I was stuck in my cocoon.""""

Buckets skipped a few. """"I heard from a coworker that his girlfriend died. He came into the café one Saturday morning. Sat at their booth. Started to cry. He didn't know me, not really, but I knew him. In time, I'd have him.""""

"*What the fuck*," Cliff mumbled, leaning in after Buckets clicked another note.

""""I waited a full week, knowing he'd come back. He did. I placed his check down on the table along with my number. I remember watching him open the piece of paper from across the café. I remember the way he looked at it—at me—like he couldn't believe I thought I had a chance with him.""""

My heart was beating out of my chest as I took the mouse from Buckets, fishing for another entry. """"But I looked just like her. We could have been twins. Why couldn't he see that?""""

I read her next statement as ice filled my veins. """"I had to make him see that.""""

Buckets chimed in. "'"'I became obsessed with my appearance.'"'"

"'"'I became obsessed with not being ugly.'"'" Cliff read. "'"'My parents became worried. They freaked when I demanded they start calling me by my middle name. I don't know why. Most of my close friends from the café called me Claire. I always hated the name Brystol, and BC was so informal.'"'"

"'"'They thought the kids at my school were bullying me. They told me we were moving and that they wanted me to get help.'"'" I glanced at the others before continuing. "'"'I thought it was a good idea. I thought it was smart to leave that town behind me, to get away, to start over.

"'"'I recommended Jefferson. I heard great things about the high school, and my parents really liked Harriet Lange.'"'"

With trembling fingers, I opened the last note in BC's portal—Discharge Diagnosis. "'There are no signs of a thought disorder. Thinking is logical and associations are intact. No signs of distress present. Judgment is generally intact. The patient says she is "better equipped to handle her emotions thanks to the wonderful doctors here." Prognosis: excellent.'"

The kitchen fell silent as I stepped away from the laptop. It wasn't long before Cliff demanded answers from me. "What the hell does all of that mean?"

"She was their waitress," I mumbled. "Jacob—he—he told me Claire used to wake him up every Saturday to try out new brunch spots around town. Butterfly Café must have been their favorite one." I dropped my head, my mind recounting a conversation from my bedroom floor. "Claire liked the butterfly effect. She must have really liked butterflies."

"So their waitress had a boner for Harrison? And what? Got rejected and got a makeover?" Cliff clasped his hands behind his head. "Is that what you're telling me?"

"She turned herself into Claire," Buckets muttered. "It's like she wasn't even pretending . . . she actually thought she *was* her."

"She probably recommended Jefferson because it was close by but far enough away." I crossed my arms and squirmed. "She must have met Guy when she was released from Harriet Lange and used him for information. Maybe he was the one who told her Jacob and I were hanging out."

"So she started following you," Buckets added.

"*Fucking* with you." Cliff slapped his water bottle into his fist, setting the record straight. "She fucked with Sonny. She framed her. And now we're in this mess because some busted girl from Long Beach couldn't handle being rejected."

"Look at this." Buckets clicked on another page, and we leaned in over his shoulders. "A list of the nursing assistants."

"Preston Hill," I mumbled. "No way . . ."

"And would you look at that . . . the guy missed his shift on the night someone torched the left wing."

"Oh my God," I whispered, realizing what that meant. "He has no alibi . . ."

“He didn’t even try to cover his tracks,” Buckets added. “With this information, we can at least point the police in his direction. Maybe they’ll get him to crack.”

“Cliff!” I grabbed his arm and smiled. “We can end this. We can clear Ari’s name!”

“Yeah . . .”

“What are you thinking?” I asked, my smile fading when I realized he wasn’t half as excited as he should have been.

Cliff took a sip from his water bottle, slowly twisting the cap back on while glaring at the screen. “I’m thinking I have a better idea.”

There will always be people who refuse to believe the black-and-white truth. Sometimes, you’ve got to give it a little color.

14 OLD HABITS

There's nothing harder to kill than an old habit. Once you become accustomed to something, you'll struggle to break out of it.

Patterns are a tricky thing. We can get so used to our own behavior—our own routines—that even if they're slowly killing us, we find them difficult to change.

But not every old habit dies hard. Worse: Some don't die at all.

"Where were you last night?"

I blinked my way back to the lunch line, turning my head to see that Kyle had joined me.

"I'm sorry; are you speaking to me now?"

"Casey told me she invited you to dinner," he whispered. "You told her you were coming."

"Something came up." I grabbed a Chicken Caesar wrap and slapped it on my tray. The days of carefully arranging my food were over. "Why do you care?"

"*She* cared."

"Look, I wanted to be there, alright? I tried to come."

Kyle grabbed two wraps and a fruit cup, following closely behind me as I walked off. "You couldn't have called? Sent a text?"

"It slipped my mind."

"Slipped your—" He huffed. "What the hell could have been so important that you couldn't show up for her?"

"Show up?" I slammed my tray down on the table, pausing to glare at him before taking my seat. "You, of all people, are going to scold me for disappointing Casey *one time*?"

"Been a little more than once."

"Back at you," I replied, removing the toothpicks.

Kyle sat down. "You see, this is *exactly* why I didn't want you hanging out with Cliff."

"What are you talking about?"

"Look at what it's doing to you!"

"It's doing nothing to me."

"You're sneaking around—"

"I'm not."

"Bailing on birthday dinners—"

"*Bailing*?"

"I'm worried about you, Sonny."

"*Now* you're worried about me?"

"I was mad at you," he reasoned.

"You kicked me out of your house, Kyle."

"And you lied to me!"

"I didn't lie!" My voice caught the attention of a few classmates. I glanced their way then tucked my chin and brought it down a notch. "Look, I shouldn't have told you I wouldn't hang out with Cliff if I knew it wasn't true, but it's not what you think it is. Maybe I appreciate his company, maybe he makes things seem less terrifying than they are, but that's it."

Kyle shook his head.

"All we're trying to do is stay two steps ahead of the situation."

"By doing what?" he asked. "What exactly is it you're doing with him?"

"Research . . ."

"Research."

"We're just—" I exhaled. "We're just trying not to get blindsided like we were with Guy Penn, alright? We're trying to figure out who this girl really was, and we're doing it for all of us."

"*You're* doing this for us," he replied. "Cliff is in this for himself."

"That isn't—"

"Listen to me, Sonny. I get you think you know him, I get you think he's helping you, but you *cannot* trust him."

"I know you believe that."

"And you don't?"

"All I know is that trusting him is my only option right now. It might not make sense to you, and you might not like it, but I'm doing *everything* in my power to make sure the situation I put myself and all my friends in doesn't come back to haunt us. I owe that to you guys, so please—" I slowly shook my head. "Please, just let me do what I need to do. If that means hanging out with Cliff, then that's just what it means."

Kyle stared into my eyes for the first time in days. "I'm just trying to protect you."

"I know that, Ky."

"You're my little sister."

It pained me to hear his voice crack, and it nearly killed me when his eyes glossed over. I stood and walked around the table, dropping down beside him for a hug. It wasn't like it usually was—warm and supportive—but it was progress.

"I just need you to trust me," I mumbled, staring over his shoulder into the crowded cafeteria. "This will all be over soon."

Later that evening, I sat at my desk in a funk, staring at a poster of BC when I should have been polishing my paper. I couldn't stop thinking about her story and how it perfectly aligned once I pieced it all together. In some sick, twisted way, I almost related. I just knew I would have been that waitress cowering in the corner of the café and wishing to God my life was as picturesque as Claire's. If I would have been the one standing there weekend after weekend watching Jacob live out his role as Prince Charming, I'm sure I would have been plagued by jealousy, too.

Maybe I would've snapped.

"Sonny! Can you get that?"

My heart raced as I lowered the poster to my lap. Fearing Guy was the person behind the doorbell, I peeked out of my bedroom window before I replied.

"Yeah!" I shouted, narrowing my eyes. "Yeah, I've got it, Dad!"

I crept down the stairs, tightening my messy bun and brushing off cracker crumbs before I opened the front door.

"Hello . . ."

"Hello . . . ?" Dean squinted at my bizarre word choice. "You're not at your mom's."

"No." I kicked myself. "No, she's, um, she's out of town for a few weeks."

He nodded, tracing my sweats and hoodie with heavy eyes. "Do you think we could talk?"

I peeked over my shoulder then closed us outside on the porch.

Dean sat down on the top step and planted his shoes on the one beneath it, staring out across the lawn. "I guess my dad realized something was up between us when you left my house the other day. He told me not to come home until I made things right."

"Been couch surfing since then?"

"Something like that." He let out a quick breath while I took my seat beside him. "I didn't know he was going to tell you what he told you."

A brief pause hung between us. I brought my knees to my chest and wrapped my arms around them. "Why didn't *you* tell me?"

"Found out right before the gala. We weren't really speaking." Dean grabbed a stick off the step and began breaking it into pieces. "I was feeling guilty about the way we ended things in my driveway. Like any good douchebag, I thought a dozen roses and knocking out your crush would win you back."

"Two dozen might've done the trick."

"Right." He huffed, the tiniest laugh breaking free. "You know, I don't even know what I was trying to accomplish that night. It's like the second Dad told me he was dating someone, the only person I could think about was you. I just—I don't know—I just wanted to talk to you so badly it almost felt like I needed to. Like I wasn't going to be okay if I didn't."

"Have you met her?" I asked, attempting to start the conversation we never had.

"No." He snapped the stick a final time and let the pieces fall. "I never want to."

"Your dad said she's pretty great."

"Yeah, I don't really give a shit."

I pressed my lips together and just watched him, listened to what he wasn't saying.

"I know what you're going to tell me," he continued. "She can't replace my mom, and I know that, but that's not stopping him from trying."

"I'm sure it feels that way."

"It feels like he's only thinking about himself."

"I get that," I whispered. "Maybe he is."

Dean rolled his head toward me.

"Maybe losing your mom made him realize life is short and that he has to live his for himself."

"And what about me? I don't matter?"

"Of course, you matter," I replied. "But you don't want your dad to be alone. It feels like that right now, it might for a while, but that's not what you really want for him." I wiped the tear off his cheek. "Is it?"

Dean sniffed and rolled his shoulders back. "Maybe I didn't want to talk to you after all."

I nudged him with my elbow as the front porch fell silent. It was a nice moment we shared—just him, me, and the elephant sitting between us.

Eventually, Dean addressed it. "Why didn't you call somebody that night?"

"Like the police?"

"Anyone," he replied. "Me, Kyle—"

"I don't know."

"You called Cliff . . . why?"

"He was just the first person I thought of."

"You two are getting pretty close . . ."

"Close?" I scoffed. "Why does everyone think Cliff and I are getting close?"

"Been hanging out a lot."

"Not for reasons you'd think," I replied.

Dean nodded then asked me the million-dollar question. "Are you—" He paused. "Are you scared?"

I buried my chin in my arms, staring across my street in a daze. "Yeah," I mumbled, watching the Peterson boys throw a football without a care in the world. "Yeah, I'm terrified."

The porch fell silent once again. I wasn't expecting Dean to admit that he was, too. I knew if I was, he'd pretend he wasn't. It's just what we did. Every scary movie we ever watched, every time the house would creak late at night, he'd always act unmoved.

We couldn't both panic.

"Sonny, listen—" He dropped his head and was onto the next thing. "I just needed you to know that our relationship falling apart is on me. It was always on me, and you have every right to date whoever you want to date."

"Maybe," I mumbled. "But I should have told you the truth about Jacob. Guess I was just trying to figure everything out myself."

"You there yet?"

"Yeah," I whispered, my stomach rolling as I wished my next words weren't true. "I like him, Dean. He's a freaking idiot . . . but I like him."

Dean nodded. I knew that was the admission he didn't want to hear but already knew. "That's funny," he mumbled, clearing his throat. "That's, uh, that's what I called you after our first fight."

"Playing basketball on my birthday was beyond selfish, and you know it."

"I was gone for two hours."

"Three, and you never said goodnight to me that night."

"Might've had something to do with your 'never speak to me again' text."

I rolled my head toward him, and we exchanged small smiles.

"I don't know what's going to happen to us now," he continued. "I'm not even sure we're going to make it out of this town, but I sure as hell hope we're still friends if we do."

"Friends?"

"Yeah." Dean's blue eyes captured mine. "If you want to be."

My arms fled toward his shoulders like they knew just where to go. I wrapped them tight around his neck while tears dripped onto his skin and whispered the only three words that mattered anymore.

"I know," he mumbled, his fingers buried in my hair. "I love you, too."

I once set out to find a passion so deep, I'd almost thought it unattainable. Just a bunch of gibberish in a journal belonging to a naive, inexperienced writer who hadn't a clue what life was really like.

But I knew if I refused to set with the sun, summer nights could bring me to the moon. And on one of those nights, I fell in love with Dean. With strawberry milkshakes on our lips and adolescent delusion in our hearts, we decided to take on the world together.

But sometimes, people change their minds. And when given the opportunity to realize it, I realized none of it—none of *us*—was enough. I wanted to feel more. I wanted to ignite. I wanted to know what it was like to yearn for someone because I was *that* sure of them.

I couldn't understand what was missing with Dean. I wasn't sure why the spark was never quite strong enough to bring us back together. And as I stared over his shoulder through my tears, I couldn't believe I wasted so much time denying *it was Jacob*.

"I should, um—" He pulled back and stood to his feet. "I should get going."

"Yeah." I wiped my face and did the same. "Call me, okay? Anytime."

Dean scanned me up and down then headed for his car, slowing his pace once he reached the middle of the lawn. "Hey!" he shouted, turning back around to face me. "Forgot!"

"Forgot . . . ?"

He tucked his chin, lifting it to pierce me once more with his misty blue eyes. "Goodnight, idiot."

"Cough twice if you're having fun at Dad's. Cough three times if you can't wait for Mom to get back."

"Is there a third option?" I asked, neck deep in bathwater.

Lana groaned. "That bad, huh?"

"Let's just say that after you left, Dad tried bonding with me over our mutual dislike for feta cheese."

"Oh God. It's worse than I thought."

"It's disastrous," I replied, switching ears. "When are you coming home again?"

"If I come home, how will you use my bathtub without permission?"

"Who said I was in your bathtub?"

"A girl just knows." Lana called for a cab in my ear.

"You know you don't actually have to yell 'taxi' to get one to stop?"

"For your information, the drivers appreciate the extra effort."

"You literally just made that up."

I heard her relay the address to her driver before buckling herself in. "So are we going to talk about it?"

"Talk about what?" I asked, pulling the drain.

"Come on, Sonny. You only soak in suds when your world is falling apart."

"I'm okay," I replied, slipping into Lana's blush silk robe. "I'd much rather talk about where you're heading off to when you have no friends."

Lana huffed. "I'll have you know I'm on a first-name basis with the guy who delivers my air filters."

"Your maintenance man?" I opened my bedroom door and reached for pajamas. "I don't know if that's sweet or sad."

"Definitely sad," she answered. "But not sadder than me heading to the grocery store solely because I ran out of cookie dough."

"I concur—that is much sadder."

"Sonny, just think! In a little over a year, you'll be in Connecticut studying your little life away, and I'll be less than two hours down the road. We'll be together again."

“Kind of,” I mumbled, pulling a big T-shirt over my head.

“It’s going to be just like old times. You and me, baking cookies . . . eating cookies . . . buying more dough . . .”

“Shamelessly hitting on maintenance men . . .”

“You won’t think it’s pathetic if he has a hot brother.”

“On that note, I’m going to bed.” My fingers met the lamp switch. “Be careful getting home.”

“I’ll call you tomorrow!”

The sound of an engine starting outside grabbed my attention. I peeked through the curtains to see Dean’s car parked on the curb, and I watched as he slowly pulled away down my street. “Yeah,” I whispered, my heart in my throat. “Talk to you then.”

Some old habits never die . . . and depending on the circumstances, that’s not always a bad thing.

15 PEACE

I can't begin to tell you the number of vacations that were ruined because of the pressure to make them peaceful. You always think that's where you'll find tranquility, don't you? While your toes are in the sand or after you've taken that first breath of fresh mountain air?

But the truth is, peace can't be planned. It's not something you can control, or schedule, or even look for. It washes over you when you least expect it . . . *where* you least expect it.

The tiny all-night diner looked like the tail end of a subway train. Its façade was painted milk-carton white, and it stood in the middle of a parking lot a hundred times its size. There were no trees, no bushes, just a dingy sidewalk that wrapped around the building and a blinking blue-and-red sign.

"You sure this will work?"

Cliff stared through his windshield, eerily calm. I wished I knew what he was thinking. From the moment Hill clocked out at Harriet Lange to the moment he bit into his burger, Cliff hadn't said a word.

I followed his lead, stepping out of the car as soon as he did. Two unlikely customers glided toward the mucky glass door, our biggest plan yet tucked just inside our back pockets.

"Pick a table," a waitress shouted, and not a soul in sight bothered to turn around. It wasn't what we were used to—it certainly was *not* a country club—but we weren't exactly in Westcott anymore.

"You ready?" Cliff muttered, his eyes on his prey.

"I'm ready," I said, my eyes on him.

But of course, I wasn't ready. How could I have been ready? What would soon take place in that red corner booth was nothing short of lunacy, the most elaborate scheme I'd ever taken part in creating. One wrong move, one slipup, and it would all blow up in our faces.

Three.

We strolled toward him, our feet light on the black-and-white speckled floor.

Two.

We reached his table, and he slowly lifted his head.

One.

"We need to talk," Cliff told him, and I slid into the booth.

Mr. Hill's eyes never moved. They stayed on Cliff like he knew they had to, and before we got around to explaining the reason for our visit, Hill dropped his napkin and leapt to his feet.

"*Don't*." Cliff stepped in front of him ever so gently so as to not draw attention. "Don't do that."

The two stood nose-to-nose, so much in common for all the wrong reasons.

"I was just leaving," Hill replied. "I'm sorry I can't stay."

"Five minutes."

"I'm sorry, Cliff, but I really can't—"

"You can," he interjected. "And you need to sit down before that waitress comes to our table assuming there's a problem."

Mr. Hill glanced toward the counter before he caved, then acted like he hadn't just tried running for his life. "What can I do for you?" he asked, sliding back into the booth.

Cliff followed, taking a moment to collect himself before the real meeting started. "We got your note."

"I'm sorry?"

"Your note," he replied. "The one you left for Lana on the night of the fire."

"To lure her to the school," I quickly added. "To frame her for arson."

"Sorry she didn't show. She'd already left for New York because she can't stand to be in town for more than a week ever since you ruined it."

Mr. Hill lost himself in Cliff's eyes, eventually reaching forward for his burger. He chomped into the bun, chewed it thoroughly, then washed it down with his shake. The slurping sound he made was out of a movie—right on cue and just menacing enough. “You wearing a wire or something?”

Cliff lifted his shirt to prove he wasn’t then followed Hill’s eyes as they traveled toward me. “Yeah, I know she’s your type, but don’t even fucking ask.”

Hill reached forward for a fry like he had all the time in the world, dunking it into honey mustard before tossing it into his mouth. “And what makes you think I wrote this note?”

“It matches the other ones you gave her,” I replied.

“Matches?”

“You folded it funny.” Cliff clenched his jaw. “That was your thing, no? The thing you had with my girlfriend?”

“My name was cleared, Mr. Reynolds. Those rumors were debunked.”

“Not because they weren’t true.”

Hill reached for another fry. “If you two have this note, why haven’t you turned me in?”

“It’s not enough,” I answered, withholding the fact that we no longer had it. “We’d need something else.”

“Like actual proof?”

“Like a timesheet showing you missed your shift that night.” Cliff shrugged. “Something like that.”

Hill grinned as he dabbed his lips with a napkin. “And how would you two know I missed my shift?”

"I'm not saying we do." Cliff leaned forward over the white tabletop. "I'm also not saying we don't, and I promise you, Preston, I'll find whatever else I have to find if you make me."

"So what do you want?" he asked, falling back with folded arms. "You want a confession?"

Cliff followed suit. "I want you to listen."

"What can I get you two?" An abrupt waitress had appeared out of nowhere, digging into her apron's deep pocket. The bottom was scalloped—a little detail I remember from that moment.

"I would love a coffee," Cliff replied, glancing at me. "You?"

"Do you happen to have green tea?"

"No," she answered matter-of-factly.

Cliff pulled out his card. "Two coffees, please."

"It's cash only after eight."

"Uh—"

"Cash. Only."

"I have cash," he said, staring blankly into her eyes. He reached into his pocket and pulled out a twenty. "Here it is. Cash."

"Give me a few minutes," she replied.

Cliff closed his eyes, rolling back to the table slightly more annoyed than before. He waited until the coast was clear to continue. "There's this girl."

"A former patient at Harriet Lange," I added. "She's missing."

"But you already knew that," Cliff continued, "because you knew BC. You used to deliver her medicine, and sometimes, she'd talk to you."

"She'd tell you stories about a guy that she liked," I offered. "A guy who didn't like her back. Eventually, you developed a tiny friendship."

"She trusted you."

I nodded. "You wanted the best for her. So when she showed up at your doorstep days after her release, you were happy to see her."

"A little surprised, given the circumstances, but you were glad she was getting ready for her first year at Jefferson."

I kept going, desperately trying to remember what we'd rehearsed. "You kept in touch. She told you she met a friend at Westcott."

"His name is Guy."

"She admitted the boy she liked was at Westcott, too."

"His name is Jacob," Cliff added.

"On the night of the fire, you weren't feeling well, so you stayed home from work."

"You were a little annoyed when BC came over unannounced, but when you saw how distraught she was, you stepped outside."

"She had just left homecoming, and Sonny was there. She told you Sonny was Jacob's new girl, and that infuriated her."

"She couldn't stand it."

Cliff shook his head. "The pretty rich girl from the rich town getting the guy."

"She told you she was going to do something about it, but you talked her down. You thought she was going home."

"You heard about the left-wing fire on the news the next morning." Cliff shrugged. "You had suspicions, so a few days later, you wrote a letter to the lead investigator, Ron Harrison. You told him about BC's obsession with his son and that you believed she may have been involved in the fire."

"You mailed it to the school."

"When they arrested Ari Ziegler, you sent another one and heard nothing."

"But when you found out BC was missing, you finally decided to call the police."

"When they ask why you're calling with this information months after the fire, you'll tell them about the letters you sent—letters that Ron Harrison will find at the bottom of a stack in his office."

"An office I have access to," I added.

Cliff leaned in. "You'll be vague with your information. BC shared some things with you but not much, so you'll encourage the police to dig into her file at Harriet Lange to corroborate your stories."

"The doctor's notes will align with everything you'll tell them and more."

"She left town—that's your best guess. She used to talk about flying away like a butterfly to a new city to start over."

"BC will go down for the fire. An unhinged girl with a well-documented obsession for Jacob Harrison fits the bill of someone who'd light his school on fire out of jealousy."

"Jealous that he and Sonny got to go there together."

"The police will rule out foul play, and most importantly, they'll start looking for a runaway instead."

"Here you go. Two coffees." The waitress placed our mugs on the table and offered Cliff his change.

"Keep it," he said, lifting his fingers, and she tucked it into her pocket.

Mr. Hill kept his head down until we were alone. When our waitress finally sauntered off, he ever so slightly glanced up, staring at us like he didn't want to know the answer to his next question. "BC," he mumbled. "Will she be flying back?"

Cliff took a sip of coffee then slowly lowered his mug. It wasn't an answer, but in the same breath, that's exactly what it was.

"Christ." Hill sighed, closing his eyes against the ugly truth. "Do you realize what you're asking me to do? You want me to pin that fire on a dead girl?"

"*Your* fire," he replied. "And I'm not asking you."

Mr. Hill gave us a good stare down, likely wondering how in the world his two former students turned into a modern-day Bonnie and Clyde. "You seriously think this will work?"

"Yeah." Cliff nodded, looking straight into the eyes of the man who hurt the only two girls he'd ever loved. "It better."

"Sonny?"

"Hi, Ms. Winchester." I peeked over her shoulder into the living room, waving at Casey's brothers who were wrestling on the couch. "Sorry to bother you."

"You're no bother," she replied, opening the door further. "Why don't you join us? We were just starting a movie."

"Actually, um—" I took a deep breath. "Is Casey home?"

"Out with Sawyer."

"Kyle?"

"Out with God-only-knows-who."

I smiled, and she lifted her popcorn as if to toast me. "Come on," she nudged. "Stay awhile."

Staying didn't seem like the worst idea. Sometimes hanging out with Mom on a Friday night is exactly what a girl needs, and if her mom is out of town, her second one is just as good.

"I guess it wouldn't be like me to turn down free popcorn," I mumbled, stepping inside.

Ms. Winchester strolled beside me toward the living room, stopping to pause the film before she walked into the kitchen. "I'll make some more."

"So you're, um—" I sat down on a barstool. "You're on babysitting duty?"

"Indefinitely."

I grinned. “How’s everything going?”

“Well, it’s been an adjustment,” she replied, reaching for a bowl. “Kyle won’t admit it, but I don’t think he likes sharing my attention with the boys.”

“That’s very ‘only child’ of him.”

“I think so, too.” She tossed a bag of kernels into the microwave. “I’m the youngest of five, so I’m used to a full house. It’s what I always wanted.”

“Got stuck with Kyle?”

“And you,” she snickered. “It’s always been just the two of you around here, and pretty soon, you’ll both be gone. It’ll be nice having some extra feet running up and down those stairs.”

“That’s a very crafty way of avoiding praises,” I replied, raising a brow to show I was serious. “You rescued them, Ms. Winchester. You saved their lives.”

“Oh, well—”

“You did,” I stopped her. “Believe me.”

She dropped her head. “I remember when Bob proposed the lottery idea. I hate to say it, but I wasn’t exactly on board.”

“No?”

“Drank a whole bottle of wine in ten minutes.”

“I guess having to pay higher tuition will do that to a person . . .”

She smiled, slowly nodding while she stared down at her velvet slippers. “I think it did the school a lot of good. Certainly brought some pretty great people there.”

"Yeah," I whispered, wondering how dreadful my life would've been had I never met Winston Banks. "I agree."

Ms. Winchester retrieved the popped corn and poured it into a bowl. "So what do you know about Kyle and Casey?"

Her words snapped me straight out of my daze.

"He's nothing like his dad was," she continued. "Since there are children around, I'll just use the words 'dead inside.'"

I smiled.

"Kyle's not afraid to be emotional, and that's why I love him. I also love that he does a terrible job at hiding things from his mother."

"Hiding things?"

"Every time that young lady walks into the room, his eyes follow her." Ms. Winchester placed the bowl in front of me and raised a brow. "That can only mean one thing."

"I, um—" I gulped, and I knew lying was pointless. "I don't think he wanted to tell you . . ."

"Mm-hmm."

"He probably thought you wouldn't have allowed them to move in."

"Well, he would have been correct."

"But they're not! He's not! I mean, Casey's with Sawyer."

"Yes, she is." Ms. Winchester grabbed both my bowl and her own and started toward the living room, tossing a kernel into her mouth along the way. "Unfortunately."

I dropped my head with a smile, widening my eyes in agreement as I pushed myself off the barstool.

The movie began, and I curled up into a ball on Kyle's chair-and-a-half. His scent lingered on the cushions, and the throw blanket I picked was the perfect size. I took a deep breath, and my body felt relaxed for the first time in months.

It knew it was home.

"Ms. Winchester?" I sounded sedated, and my eyes were barely open as I stared straight ahead at the foyer.

She turned her head with a smile, curled up under a blanket of her own. "Yes, Sonny?"

"Why do your favorite flowers look like freaky little monkeys?"

Peace can wash over you anywhere, on a sheet of white sand or during an animated movie in the middle of your best friend's living room while chatting about flowers from mountainous rainforests in southeastern Ecuador. You have to take what you can get.

16 SERVICE HOURS

"Scoot." Winston dropped onto the bus bench.

I shimmied toward the window, rolling my eyes at his camel-colored faux fur coat. "You look like you just walked out of 1979."

"Thank you," he replied.

"Not a compliment."

"Definitely a compliment." Winston removed his cloak, putting his weight on me to make the process easier. "Have any gummy bears?"

"Oh, yeah, sure." I shoved him off. "Let me just dig into my stash real quick."

"You have a stash?"

"No." I squinted. "That was sarcasm."

"Well, knock it off! I have to find some sugar, *stat*."

"Didn't you eat breakfast?"

"Two bagels and a cranberry-orange muffin isn't going to hold me." He bobbed his head up and down in search of sweets. "Not on a day like today."

Westcott students looked forward to the weekends the most, but on that specific Saturday, activity buses were filled with kids wishing Monday would hurry up. The time had come to put in our annual service hours, and nothing said "we're here to help" like a bunch of Violets who didn't know how to hold a hammer.

"What do they have us doing this time?" I mumbled.

Winston tore into a bag of fruity vitamins he snagged from someone else's bag. "I think we're restoring an old building."

I pressed my lips together and nodded. "You've reached a new low."

"Speaking of low, how's Jacob?"

"Jacob?"

"I heard he's taking Alice Kennedy to Reels next weekend." Winston popped a lime green dinosaur into his mouth. "He moves on faster than my mom's therapists."

"You don't know that he moved on," I replied. "He's probably just trying to make me jealous."

"Is it working?"

"Like a charm." I stared out the window, watching as Guy stepped onto the bus beside ours. "You know, someone asked me to Reels, too."

Winston choked on his gummy.

"Don't die," I continued. "It was just Guy Penn."

"Guy asked you on a date?"

"Not exactly. He wants to *talk*."

"Have you told anyone this?"

"Not yet." I glanced back out the window as Cliff climbed onto the third bus. His hood covered his head, but his sparkling-white sneakers gave him away. "I wasn't sure if it was worth mentioning."

"You weren't sure we'd want to know the freak-of-the-week has the hots for you?"

"That's not what it is," I dismissed. "He's just trying to intimidate me. He wants me to believe he knows more than he does and that I should agree to a conversation with him."

"Speaking of freaks . . ."

I followed Winston's gaze toward the aisle where Norah's middle finger was waiting for him.

"Classy," he hollered as she stalked to the back, then he turned to roll his eyes at me. "Daddy issues, am I right?"

"Seriously?"

"You guys won't believe this." Kyle dropped into the adjacent bench. "Cliff copped to his injury."

"English," Winston barked.

"He told Coach he was hurt. He's—he's out." I watched as Kyle struggled to make sense of it, knowing I could easily clear it up. But Cliff's demand to not tell Kyle about the deal he made with Sawyer laid heavy on my mind, so I sat back and watched him try to connect the dots on his own. "I thought he was going to keep that from him . . ."

"Maybe he realized he shouldn't," I suggested.

"Yeah." He squinted. "Maybe."

"You two friends again?" Winston asked, and Kyle and I exchanged a look. "Is that a yes . . . ?"

The bus driver took off down the road, setting our dreadfully long day into motion and becoming the perfect distraction. I wasn't sure what was going on between Kyle and myself—or with any of my friends, for that matter. We were in this weird limbo, a waiting game, and no one really knew what to think about me.

I couldn't blame them. I didn't know what to think about me either.

"Where were you last night?"

Kyle rolled his head my way. "What do you mean?"

"I stopped by, and you weren't home."

"Oh, I was—" He ran his fingers over his eyes and dragged them down his face. "I was on a run."

"For three hours?"

His eyes narrowed.

"I stayed and watched a movie with your mom."

"Well, had I known that, I would have adjusted my story."

"Talk about lying," I quipped. "Seriously, where were you?"

"It's not important."

"It wasn't before you lied about it."

Kyle sighed. "I was at Ari's, okay?"

"Oh God." Winston lifted his eyes and hands to the sky, tossing the vitamin bag into the seat behind him. "Take me, Lord, I'm ready."

"It's not what you think," Kyle explained, reaching down to collect his trash. "I just wanted to talk to her."

"About what?"

"The investigation," he replied. "I hadn't checked on her since she lost her hearing. I was just curious to know what was going on with everything."

I wasn't sure I believed that—not entirely anyway. "So how is she?"

"Pretty bad."

"Worse than usual?" Winston asked.

"She's different," Kyle replied. "She's . . . softer?"

"Softer?"

"Yeah, softer, nicer, I don't know how to explain it. It's—it's almost like she's given up."

"That doesn't sound like Ari . . ."

"No, it doesn't," he agreed. "She looks like she's lost weight and hasn't slept in days."

"Doesn't she always look like she hasn't slept in days?" Winston asked, and I nudged him in the gut. "What? I'm just trying to keep him honest."

“Everything will work out,” I assured him, knowing the implementation of our plan to pin the fire on BC was right around the corner—a plan no one could know existed until it was carried out.

“Yeah.” Kyle nodded. “Hope so.”

“Back to more pressing news.” Winston reached down and grabbed a missing person poster off the mucky bus floor. “We’re two pokes of a pirate’s sword away from falling off the plank into cement cells.”

“Colorful.”

“Guy reprinted,” he continued. “I know this one is from his second batch because the paper’s thicker.”

“He wants to find her.”

“He wants to nail us,” Winston replied. “And possibly some of us in more than one way.”

Kyle scrunched his entire face. “What the fuck?”

“He has the hots for Sonny.”

“He does *not* have the hots for me, okay?”

Kyle’s mouth fell open comically. “Wait, *Guy Penn* likes you?”

“He asked me to go to Reels with him,” I explained. “He said he wanted to talk. It wasn’t a romantic thing, believe me.”

“Hang on—talk?” Kyle searched up and down the aisle before leaning closer. “You think he knows something?”

My eyes once again hit the glass, the aesthetic pleasure of trees whipping by doing little to soothe me. “It won’t matter soon," I whispered to myself, playing out our plan in my mind. Once the story broke, Guy would have no choice but to believe the police and their findings, and he'd be off our backs for good.

We just had to stay calm. BC just had to stay hidden. Hill just had to make one little call, and we'd finally be free.

But none of that was as easy as it sounded, and as we took a left turn into a massive vacant parking lot, I was beginning to think we'd never be unchained.

You know those moments in life where something so out of the ordinary happens that your cheeks begin to burn? That your body tingles from head to toe? When terror pricks at you, and before you know it, you've convinced yourself that it's the end?

Yeah. Me, too.

2874 Baker Street had called us back, and not just us . . . *the entire junior class of Westcott High*.

"Mr. Harrison!" I spoke with authority from my gut but still managed to sound as scared as I was. The surrounding conversations diminished, and the entire bus was looking at me. "Where—where are we going?"

Ron, one of many chaperones that morning, swiveled in his seat. "To serve!"

"But where? *Here*? Why—why here?!"

"We'll explain all of that in a minute, Ms. Carter." The driver put the bus in park, and through the grimy windshield, the abandoned warehouse stared me dead in my soul. "You kids stay put. I'm going to speak with the other chaperones before we unload."

"Mr. Harrison, wait!" I felt a firm grip around my wrist, and Winston pulled me down.

"What the hell are we doing here?" he whispered, his voice shaking like a leaf. "*This* is the building we're restoring?"

"What do we do, Ky?" I cried, tears filling my eyes quicker than I could get rid of them.

"I don't know." He pressed the side of his glossy forehead against the brown leather. "I—I can't think straight."

"The blood . . . the blood on the concrete . . ."

"Shit." Kyle closed his eyes, prompting more tears to fill mine. "I forgot about that."

"Maybe it'll pass as an oil stain," Winston offered.

"An oil stain? *Really*?!"

"Alright, ladies and gentlemen, let's get out there!" Ron shouted, tapping each student on the shoulder as they exited the bus.

The three of us tarried, hiding behind the benches in front of ours in hopes that we could come up with a plan in the following twenty seconds.

"I can pull the fire alarm," I offered.

Kyle nodded. "That's not a bad idea."

"Here's a better one," Winston replied. "I'm going to rip all my clothes off in a psychotic break and run sprints around the parking lot. Sonny's going to chase after me, fall, twist her ankle, and belt out a bloodcurdling scream. Kyle, fearing your friend is gravely injured, you're going to pick her up, pull your back out, puke—just a little; don't overdo it—and the chaperones will have no other choice but to call the whole thing off and take us to the hospital."

"Are you out of your mind?" I hissed. "Neither of us can run!"

"I'm missing three students!" Ron shouted.

We collectively sighed and stood to our feet.

"Ah! Three of my favorites!" He waved a hand at us. "Let's go, let's go."

One by one, we left the bus. My sneaker hit the ground, and I immediately felt like I'd stepped into an alternate reality. Like I was a character in my own video game, just standing there waiting for someone else to move me.

Cliff appeared in my peripheral vision. I turned my head just as he was stepping off his bus, and our eyes immediately found each other's. He softly shook his head as if to warn me not to walk toward him.

Piper slowly passed by me. Her arms were crossed over her burgundy hoodie, and her matching burgundy yoga pants paired nicely with the pool of dried blood on the cement merely twenty feet away. She joined the circle of students then casually turned her head and locked eyes with me.

"Come on." Buckets wrapped his hand around my arm and pulled me forward.

"But—"

"I know." He swallowed. "We all know."

Colors swirled all around me as we sauntered toward the warehouse. I knew I was surrounded by classmates, but I couldn't make out their faces. Everything was moving too fast—everything was spiraling out of control.

I called out for Buckets, but my pleas must've gotten lost. He wasn't stopping—he was pulling us closer. He was pulling us toward the stain.

I didn't want to see it. I didn't want to stand there. Why wasn't he stopping? Where were we going? *Where were we*?

"Hey." He squeezed my shoulders, and my eyes eventually landed on his face. "Listen to me, okay? Guy's watching us, and if we give him a reason to, he's going to realize something's up. Everything we do right now matters. Everything we say. You have to calm down."

"But—"

"We're going to stand on it."

"Buckets—"

"Just to hide it," he replied. "Trust me."

Without looking down, we took a step forward. Knowing I was standing on top of BC's innards made my chest heave, and though he was trying to play it cool, I knew Buckets was having a similar reaction. "Just keep looking at me." He groaned, and so I did. "We just have to get through this day, that's all."

"What if someone walks into the woods?"

"They shouldn't," he replied. "Not *that* far."

"What if they do? What if someone finds her?"

"They won't."

"We had everything planned," I mumbled under my breath. "We had everything planned. We had everything—"

"Alright, everyone gather 'round!"

Buckets nodded. I nodded. We turned to face the day.

Mr. Harrison lifted his palms to the sky and moved his fingers up and down, attempting to pull us closer. "Today, you've been assigned the wonderful job of restoring this old warehouse. Some of you may know this used to be a grocery store back in the day, but it's since been purchased by a nonprofit here in Westcott whose mission is to build homes for the less fortunate."

"Cobalts," someone coughed, setting off a rumbling of laughter.

"This warehouse will be used to store lumber, building materials, and appliances, so we don't need to get it perfect, but we need to clear it out and give it a little makeover. Any questions?" Ron nodded when no one spoke up. "Great! Come grab a checklist, and let's get to work!"

SERVICE HOURS: PART TWO

"Enjoying the view?"

Wavy red hair reflected in the sun as I jumped at the voice. I whipped my head to the right, dropping a pile of screws in the process. "Jesus, Alice! Could you not?"

"Sorry?" She joined me behind the long row of plastic folding tables set up in the parking lot, supposedly a solid place for supplies, but the rolling hardware would've disagreed. I rushed around the table to grab a cluster of nails before they plummeted to the concrete.

"Aren't you on sweeping duty?" I asked, kneeling to collect a few escapees. Between Alice's legs, I caught a clear shot of the *oil stain* thirty feet away, and my heart began to pound.

"I was," she answered, rearranging my piles while staring ahead at the warehouse. "But I think I like your job better."

"I don't think that's how this works."

"No?"

"No," I replied, making my way back behind the table. I followed her gaze and noticed she was gawking at the hardworking guys—one in particular.

"Jacob's taking me to Reels next weekend," she bragged, twirling her red locks around her finger.

I glanced his way and watched him balance a sheet of plywood on his head.

"I know you guys have a thing," she continued. "Just wanted to make sure it was alright with you before we went."

At that moment, I was certain Alice's surprise table visit was more to boast than to beg. "If we had a thing, don't you think he would've said no?"

"Oh, yeah." She smiled, dropping her hair with a shrug. "I guess you're right."

My eyes widened.

"Before I forget, you *have* to tell me where you got that dress you wore to the gala. The navy-blue one with the high slit?" She pinched her fingers together and lifted them in the air. "Literally so gorgeous."

"Thanks . . ." I glanced beyond her shoulder toward the woods.

"The name?"

"Uh . . . Olivia's . . . Olivia's Closet."

"Perfect! I'll look it up!"

Suddenly, Mr. Harrison blocked my view. "Alice, where are you supposed to be?"

"At the warehouse?"

"Back to your station," he replied, and she sauntered off, grumbling. But she didn't get far, because I just couldn't do it—bite my tongue and pretend she hadn't turned into the exact person she swore she wouldn't become.

"Hey, Alice?"

She whipped around, lifting her perfectly plucked brow to the morning sky.

"Way to keep your promise!" I shouted, furrowing mine, and her face slowly dropped.

"Alright, go on," Ron said, urging her to leave, but our gaze was hard to break. I could tell I'd struck a nerve, touched a sore spot, and that's exactly what I wanted to do.

Alice eventually turned around and walked off toward the other side of the parking lot, leaving me there to wonder what she would've said had Ron not been there. "I see that girl bothers you as much as she does me."

"She doesn't bother your son," I replied, still heated.

"I heard about that," he mumbled. "Was sort of hoping I'd heard wrong."

"He's taking her to Reels next weekend, so . . ."

"I heard right, then?"

I nodded.

"Well, I just might have to find a reason to ground him."

"It's alright." A smile crept to my lips, and I changed the subject. "Hey, listen—I was actually just about to come find you . . ."

"Oh?"

"I wanted to ask if I could swing by your office Monday morning?"

"Is this about your paper?"

"I'm afraid so."

"Never-ending," he replied. "Making another change?"

I nodded, and the plan to plant Mr. Hill's letters was in motion. "I'll be in and out in five minutes. You have my word."

"Swing by," he succumbed. "I'd like to talk to you about something as well."

"Me?" I swallowed. "You want to talk to me?"

"I've been thinking a lot about what you said the night you stopped over. There are a few things I'd like to ask you."

"Mr. Harrison, I—"

"Swing by." His eyes whispered a thousand questions, but I couldn't make out any of them. "We'll talk Monday."

I dropped my head, only lifting it once I heard him start a conversation with another student. Unfortunately, the person walking toward me when I looked up was no better.

"Has anyone noticed the stain?" Norah whispered angrily.

"Not that I know of."

"Well, are you watching?"

"In between trying to act normal, yes!"

She clenched her jaw. "Go to your friend. I'll stand in."

"My friend?"

"Casey," she answered. "She's around back throwing up."

I heard whispers of affirmations as I approached the end of the metal wall, glancing behind my shoulder to ensure a teacher hadn't followed me here. As I got closer, I recognized the soothing voice and decided to take a back seat.

"Deep breaths," Kyle whispered as I came to a halt, peeking my head around the edge of the building.

Casey was hunched over a pile of brush, dry-heaving her guts out.

"Just take some deep breaths," he continued, rubbing his hand up and down her back.

"I feel like I'm dying."

"You're not dying," he replied. "Being back here just has you scared, that's all."

"I—I can't—I can't breathe."

"You can."

"It doesn't feel like I can."

"If I can breathe, you can breathe," he replied. "I'm right here with you, alright?"

Kyle stood beside her, offering his support. He never rushed her to stand up or forced her to stop crying—he just waited for her to realize she was okay.

That took another five minutes.

Casey stood. She wiped her tears with the help of Kyle, and as soon as his hand touched her cheek, her eyes shot to his, her gaze tortured.

"We should—" He pulled his thumb off her face. "We should head back."

But the two of them stood there like they weren't convinced they should. Like there were so many things left unsaid between them. Like they needed to talk, like they wanted to, but the circumstances forbid it.

"Yeah," she replied, shaking off the spell. "Yeah, Sawyer's probably wondering where I am."

Kyle nodded, and I ran for my life when I saw them coming.

I couldn't understand where everything went wrong, and maybe too many things had. Between Ari and Sawyer and Ms. Winchester's blurry house rules, it was hard to pinpoint the exact reason for their demise.

I wondered if they even knew.

"*Jesus*!" I shouted, jumping back before I took an entire pail of paint water to the chest.

"Whoa!" Guy pulled the bucket closer to him, his eyes wide. "In a hurry?"

"Kind of."

He glanced behind my head. "You guys aren't having a party back there, are you?"

"A party?" My eyes narrowed as he inched his way toward the woods. "Where—where are you going?"

"To dump this," he answered.

"In there?"

"Indeed."

"But isn't there paint inside?"

"A little."

"Well, won't that stain the sticks?"

Guy stopped in his tracks, mere feet away from entering the oaks. "Are you being environmentally conscious or just concerned it'll look bad?"

"That depends. Which one will mean you won't go in there and dump it?"

"Neither, considering I was told to." He took a step forward. "For aesthetics' sake, I'll make sure I walk it back some."

"Wait!"

But he didn't.

"Guy, wait!" I shouted.

And he waddled on.

"I—I wanted to tell you something!"

Bucket in hand, he turned around.

"I, um—"

"You what?"

"It's just that I was thinking, well, I was sort of re-thinking—"

"My arms are turning to jello, Sonny; could you land the plane?" He ever so slightly turned toward the trees, and in a knee-jerk reaction, I blurted out the biggest lie yet. "I'd like to go to Reels with you!"

Guy's narrowed eyes slowly opened. "Is that so?"

I shrugged, neck-deep in regret. "Yeah. Why not?"

Two seconds too late, Dean scooped the pail from his hands. "Jesus, Guy, we told you to dump this ten minutes ago."

He watched Dean perform his job for him then grinned at me before returning to his station. "Pick you up at seven."

I nodded, squeezing my eyes shut the second he walked away. I'd just agreed to a conversation with the guy who suspected we were involved in the disappearance of his best friend, and what made matters worse?

I was.

"Cliff!" His eyes followed my voice and found me standing near the paint cans. "I have that roller you were asking for!"

"One sec!" he replied, hopping down off a ladder. Taking his sweet time, he strolled toward me with a splash of *dulce de leche* on his hoodie. "Thanks for this."

A few classmates walked by us, and we waited until they were out of earshot before we dropped the act.

"What the fuck were you doing over there with Guy Penn?!"

"Oh, so you *did* see that?"

"Should I have jumped off the ladder and sprinted there?" he asked, swiping his sleeve across his sweaty forehead.

"That would have done less damage than I just did," I shot back. "I just agreed to a date with him!"

"A date? What are you talking about?"

"He dropped by my house the night we hacked into Harriet Lange and asked me to go to Reels with him next weekend."

"And you said yes?"

"I said no until he was two seconds away from walking into the woods. I was trying to distract him!"

"That's what you came up with?" Cliff kneeled and sorted through the paint cans. "He wants to get you alone."

I joined him. "I'm planting the letters first thing Monday morning. If Hill calls on Tuesday, that'll give the police a few days to look into his claims. Come Friday, news will have spread, and Guy will probably be too distracted to even think about going to Reels."

"And if not?"

"Then I play stupid like I've been doing."

"Not very well," he shot back. "One slipup, and you unravel our entire story. No fucking way we're risking that."

"Look, let's just take one day at a time, okay?"

He stood to his feet, a paint can he never needed dangling from his fingers.

"Yo, Reynolds!"

“Yo,” he shouted at his buddy while glaring down at me.

“Can you go check on Harrison?!”

“Where’s he at?” Cliff asked.

“Not sure! I think he went to dump paint!”

SERVICE HOURS: PART THREE

I wasn't sure how it happened, or how quickly or how slow, but I was almost eye level with Cliff before I had time to process what was said.

We whipped our heads toward the woods, but Jacob was nowhere in sight. Panic surged through me, and Cliff grabbed my arm in a last-ditch attempt to keep control. "Walk slowly toward the side of the warehouse. Once you're around the wall, book it twenty feet then turn for the woods. Run straight for a while, then take a left and come up behind him."

"Cliff—"

"*Go*," he groaned.

My feet swept me away before I could argue; maybe they understood the severity of the situation before I did. Paint fumes pushed against my face as I glided toward the side of the building, and I prayed a chaperone wouldn't stop me before I could get there. My eyes were glued to the woods, desperately trying to spot Jacob, but all that stood before me were blurry brown lines.

I reached the edge of the warehouse then booked it twenty feet like Cliff had said, giving enough space between myself and the parking lot full of people. Once I was far enough away, I took a sharp left turn and ran for my life.

Focus, I thought, glancing sideways every few seconds.

How could we be so unlucky?

How could the one thing we were trying to avoid be happening?

How could nine people fail to guard one lot?

My eyes landed on Jacob and the full horror of the situation amidst the trees. He swiveled on the sticks, marching toward the parking lot like he had something to share. Before he could, I wrapped my hand around his mouth and pulled him back against my chest.

He peeled my fingers away and spun around, his eyes narrowing when he saw me holding another one over my lips.

"Sonny? What the hell are you—"

"Shh." A tear fled from my eye and dropped to the leaves below. I could smell them, musky and sweet.

"Not now," he continued. "I have to find my dad. I—I just found—"

"I know," I replied, refusing to turn around. If I saw her, it was real and not something my friends and I left behind on some street called Baker.

"You *know*? You know what?"

There was no misinterpreting the pain in my eyes—he just had to stare a little longer to figure it out. "Sonny?"

I felt like he wanted me to say it.

"What are you trying to say?"

I felt like he needed to hear it.

With nothing left to do, I gave our secret one last squeeze and let go.

"If you go out there right now and tell your dad what you found, I'll be arrested."

Jacob's narrowed eyes slowly widened. "You're joking . . ."

"No." I placed my trembling fingertips on the torrent of tears that had soaked my face. "But I really wish I were."

The wind picked up, disturbing the trees like we'd done that cold, horrific night. It swept between us and blew my hair onto my cheek, and I was far too numb to move it.

"What are you telling me?" he asked. "That you—that you knew that girl was lying there?"

"'That girl' has a name."

He waited.

"BC," I whispered.

He squinted. "The girl from Jefferson?"

"The girl from Butterfly Café."

The wind blew once again—good news for the wet paint but bad for me. My teeth began to chatter as if a ghost had joined us. I suppose, in a way, one had.

"How do you know about that?" he mumbled, like he didn't want me to know. Like the café was *theirs*—his and Claire's—not ours. His to hold, not mine. Like all the memories it held belonged to them.

"She was your waitress," I whispered. "Your waitress from the café. She must have waited on you and Claire, and she watched you, and she fell in love with you."

"What are you talking about?" he spat.

"After Claire died, a server slipped you her number, do you remember?"

A quick flicker in his eyes told me he did.

"*Son*?"

Ron's voice flew through the branches. I jumped up on my toes and grabbed Jacob's arms, pleading for his pity most pitifully. "Look, I'll explain everything, I swear! Just don't say anything!"

"Explain what?"

"I—"

"Did you—" He squinted. "Did *you* kill her?"

"Son?" Ron's voice drew near. "Son, you in there?"

"Please," I pleaded. "Please, you have to go!"

"Answer my question."

"Jacob, please!"

He grabbed my face; his breathing quickened. From afar, you would've thought we were seconds away from kissing, and God, I wished that were the case. "Answer me." He pressed his fingers into my skin. "Did you kill her?"

My eyes instinctively closed. Whatever he saw in them when I looked up must've answered his question. He slowly released me—us—and he took a step back as if he couldn't stand standing next to me.

Ron called for him once more, and judging from the sound of his voice, he'd entered the woods. My entire life was in Jacob's hands, and I didn't take that as lightly as one might assume. Things hadn't been the same between us, and I wasn't sure what he was going to do.

"Yeah!" Jacob shouted, dragging his glare off me and toward the warehouse. "Yeah, Dad, I'm coming!"

As he left me there with her, the irony wasn't lost on me. A girl flying high who had nothing to lose ten feet from one neck-deep who stood to lose everything. Oddly enough—I wasn't sure which was worse.

17 LOOSE ENDS

The day I realized we humans have no idea what we're doing was the day I was free. Unlimited advice is at our fingertips, all given by people who are just taking their best guess on the situation. Because that's all we can do, really—*guess*. We live, and we love, and we make mistakes, but at the end of the day, nobody really knows how to fix them. We're all just running around putting out little fires . . . we're all just tying up loose ends.

How does a person walk the packed halls of their high school at seven thirty AM with two incriminating letters in their backpack and a wicked plan on their mind? They can't.

So they get there at seven.

"You're here early this morning." Ms. Pamela greeted me with a smile—one I didn't deserve.

"I'm supposed to be meeting Mr. Harrison?"

"That explains it," she replied. "I believe the janitor just left his office, so it should be unlocked. You can wait in there if you'd like."

"Thanks." I made my way, clenching my book bag's straps so tightly my fingers were turning white.

"Oh, and Sonny?"

"Yes?" I glanced back.

"Keep the door open."

I pressed my lips together and continued my journey, deciding right then and there I needed to be particularly cautious. These weren't just any letters. They were letters that couldn't be explained had someone caught me planting them.

I reached his office door and gently pushed it open. The poorly lit room smelled like cleaning products, but Ron's grassy, sweet cologne lingered. His coffee mug had held down the fort all weekend long, and I wondered if he was searching for it at home. It looked like the kind of mug that would be someone's favorite—stoneware with a large handle, something out of his mother's cabinet.

Ms. Pamela hopped on a phone call, and I took that as my opportunity to shuffle through his belongings in peace.

Just where I'd put those letters was the question. On the bookshelf? In a drawer? Should I have used the last drop of coffee in his mug as glue and pressed the envelope against an old piece of mail? A thousand ideas fought to take first place; I just didn't know which one deserved it.

I dallied with my thoughts as I strolled toward Ron's desk. My mind shifted, however, as it became clear that every drawer was locked. The sudden realization caused me to panic. His office wasn't only dark and sparkling clean, it was small, too, and the hiding spots were disappearing before my eyes.

But a nearby frame on the shelf behind Ron's desk saved the day. Beneath it was a rather large stack of envelopes—some open, some sealed—and it looked like a pile where overlooked letters would live.

With a glove on my hand, I reached into my bag and lifted Hill's handwritten messages. My stomach churned just staring at them, but I sojourned on—I had to.

Part of me wondered what Lana ever saw in him. The guy had caused so much damage, ruined so many lives, but then again, who was I to judge?

I shoved the letters in between the others—one toward the top, one toward the bottom—then proudly pulled my glove off like I'd just performed a lifesaving surgery. I wasn't only pleased that I'd planted them successfully, I was also thrilled that I remembered to wear the glove.

Just then, the frame called me back. I brought it to my face and crumbled when I realized who it was. A young Jacob, maybe ten, holding a fish the size of his entire arm. I wondered what that little boy was thinking at that exact moment. Oddly enough, I wouldn't have to wait long to find out.

"Biggest one caught that day."

A voice rolled into my eardrum, but I never flinched. It wasn't there to sneak up on me, and somehow, my soul knew that.

"You looked happy," I mumbled, my back to him.

"I was."

The click of the office door prompted me to turn around. Jacob was there to greet me, leaning against the wall with dead eyes and nothing to say.

I let out the breath I'd been holding in for a minute, but no words came out with it. If there were ever a time words didn't matter, it was right there in that office at seven fifteen. "Where's your dad?"

"Had to stop by the station," he replied, and the room became quiet. I even noticed sounds I hadn't before. Like a continual thud in the vent above my head and a tapping noise in the wall behind me.

"I guess you want an explanation?"

Jacob shrugged like it was all he could do. "How do you explain something like that?"

Shame forced my head lower. It was one thing for Cliff to know I'd done something terrible or for Kyle to know or JC. But Jacob was still so new to it all—Westcott and its unforgiving ways—and he couldn't possibly understand how I'd come to that decision.

"You don't." I shrugged like him. "I can't *explain* what I've done, but I can tell you what happened."

And so it began . . . the story that seemed so unbelievable, I'd almost convinced myself it wasn't true.

The clock ticked, but we never ran out of time, and we never ran into Ron. Within minutes, Jacob knew it all—such a small word that packs such a punch.

"I can't tell you how, but within a few days' time, the fire will be pinned on her, they'll assume she fled, and this will all be over."

Jacob walked toward me. Up until then, he'd kept his spot against the wall warm while I'd stood near a photo of him and a catfish. "Why would you think I lied about Claire?"

"I told you," I answered. "The way BC introduced herself at the bakery, I thought she—"

"—was my dead ex-girlfriend?"

"Jacob—"

"I told you Claire was dead. Why didn't you just come to me? We could have confronted this girl together."

"I—"

"You don't trust me," he replied. "It's why you thought I lied about Claire's death, and it's why you accused me of trying to lure you to that parking lot on the night of the fire. You don't—you don't trust me, Sonny."

"You've lied before," I cautiously fired back.

"About stupid shit, about things I wasn't allowed to talk about—"

"I screwed up."

"You've done more than that." Jacob shook his head. "This isn't about you and me, or where we stand, or what's happened between us—that's meaningless compared to what's going on right now."

"I know."

"Do you know the situation you've put me in? My dad works for the police department, Sonny. If he finds out I knew—"

"You don't know anything," I replied. "You have nothing to do with this."

"I have everything to do with this. I saw her body and said nothing."

"Nobody knows that."

"*I* know it." Jacob cupped his mouth and paused. "How am I supposed to sleep at night knowing this girl followed her crush to a new town and got herself killed for it?"

"Please, don't—"

"What? Humanize her? She was a *person*."

"Of course, she was!"

"She didn't deserve this."

"You think I don't know that?! I have spent *every day* since that night asking myself how innocent Sonny Carter could do what she did. Do you honestly believe for one second that I don't realize it was wrong?!"

"I want to help you, Sonny, but I don't know how." Jacob's voice cracked. "Tell me how to help you."

"You can play dumb," I replied, a tear fleeing from my eye. "When the cops question you, you can tell them exactly what you just told me—you didn't really know her."

He slowly shook his head, and I realized he was going to be the most willing unwilling participant there was. "You want me to lie to the police?"

"It's not a lie, is it?"

"It's an omission."

"Look, you asked how you can help me." I shrugged. "This is how."

Jacob took a long, hard look at me. "All this time, I thought you were acting strange because you were still in love with Dean. You let me believe that, Sonny—you let me believe I wasn't what you wanted."

"Had I told you what was going on, would it have changed anything?"

"It would have changed everything!"

"Would it have stopped you?" I asked.

"Stopped me from what?"

"Running to Alice?"

His face dropped. "Sonny, Alice means nothing to me."

"You don't typically save love notes from people who mean nothing to you. Believe me—" I yanked open the door. "I would know."

I'd walked by his locker a thousand times, stopped at it a dozen, but that morning, I was hesitant to look his way. I felt like we were the only two people who knew a bomb was about to go off. Well, two out of four.

"Mr. Harrison never showed," I whispered, wondering why.

Cliff cut his eyes at me while dumping books into his backpack. It hung on the little metal latch since he only had one functioning arm. "Did you get it done or not?"

"By the grace of God."

"I wouldn't bring Him into this," Cliff replied. "Where'd you put them?"

"In a pile."

"A good one?"

"Yeah, it was beautiful." I rolled my eyes. "Is everything still on for tomorrow?"

"First thing," he replied. "What does Jacob know?"

"Oh, you know, just a little short of everything."

Buckets joined us not a moment too soon. Something about his involvement made everything seem a little less psychotic. "Did you plant the letters?"

I nodded.

"Knock on wood, but I think we're going to pull this off," he replied, taking a swig from his energy drink.

"When you say 'knock on wood,' you're actually supposed to."

Buckets tapped Cliff's textbook and received a particularly cutting glare.

Cliff turned his attention on me. "Is Harrison going to be a problem?"

"I don't think so," I answered.

"You need to be sure."

"Look, we aren't exactly on the best of terms right now. I'm not sure of anything when it comes to him."

Buckets tossed me a buoy. "I don't think Jacob will talk. I—I could be wrong, but I don't think I am."

Cliff nodded, though I wasn't sure that was going to be enough. He drifted away into his sea of Violet friends while I stayed behind with a blue one. All was as it should be.

"How's Hannah?" I asked, peeling my eyes off his letterman jacket.

Buckets cleared his throat. "Good. She's been eying this glittery coat in a store window for like three weeks now. I surprised her with it when she got home from the hospital."

His reply sucked a smile from me. Even I was shocked to feel it—*joy*. "Did it fit?"

He shrugged like a proud, slightly embarrassed big brother would do. "I guess."

"Well, I'm sure she was very surprised."

"She's a punk, that kid. Cost triple what I thought it would."

"As things that sparkle do." For a brief moment, I'd forgotten my outlook on life was supposed to be hopeless. "I, um—" I dropped my head. "I should go grab my books before the bell rings."

"Yeah." He nodded, realizing the same. "Keep me posted, okay?"

I started toward my locker, but a tug on my heartstrings spun me back around. "Hey, Buckets?"

He quickly looked up, almost like he too felt the conversation wasn't over.

"Thank you . . ." I told him, unsure of why he ever agreed to help someone like me. "For everything."

My feet smacked against the track like bricks yet again. I was no longer questioning the sanity of the person who claimed it relieved stress—I was questioning Kyle's and why he ever thought his warehouse shenanigans were a good idea.

To say I was glaring at his back while he jogged in front of me was an understatement—I was trying to burn a hole through it.

Like a track-team reject with something to prove, I sprinted my heart out and managed to catch him. "You are such a moron."

"Hi to you, too," he replied, not even half as out of breath as I was.

"You can't do it again."

"Do what?"

"Comfort Casey." I was falling behind, so thankfully my words stopped him in his tracks—literally. "I saw you two behind the warehouse."

"How could you have seen that?"

"I'm asking the questions here," I answered, pressing against the shooting pain in my ribcage. "What's going on, Ky? You said your mom won't allow the two of you to be together."

"She won't."

"You said you weren't going to come between her and Sawyer."

"I'm not."

"That's not what it looked like back at the warehouse!"

Classmates zipped by us, and then there was Winston.

"I was just checking on her," he explained. "I was being a friend."

"You were wiping her tears."

"Friends can do that." He sighed when he realized I didn't buy it. "Look, what do you want me to say? I'm trying to navigate this the best way I know how."

"By cashing in on her panic attack?"

His eyes narrowed. "You can't seriously think that's what I was doing?"

"I think you're crossing a line."

Kyle tightened the drawstring on his joggers and looked up. "I'm sorry—are you campaigning for her and Sawyer now?"

"No, Ky, but what you're doing isn't right! Rubbing her back? Whispering into her ear?"

"You're overreacting."

"I'm trying to protect her!" I shouted. "Because if you can't pursue her, for whatever reason, then you have to let her go!"

His eyes shot to mine, but he wasn't really seeing me. His mind was somewhere else, on something else—he was gone.

"Look, I'm just trying to help," I mumbled, attempting to backpedal. "You know you have to do this."

But he didn't respond.

"Ky—" I stepped forward, but he stepped back. "Ky, it's the right thing to do."

He hit the ground with the flat of his foot, and he looked me over once more before taking off down the track.

The right thing, maybe, but not the easiest . . . *walking away is never that.*

"We keep missing each other."

"But how could I miss you here?" Casey asked, inching her way toward her clunker. Seeing me sitting on it was, I'm sure, the last thing she expected to see after school. "Genius."

"Or weird."

"It's definitely that," she replied, tossing her book bag in the trunk. "Did you need a ride home?"

"Nope."

"Did you just want to hang out on the hood of my car . . . ?"

"Kind of." I scrunched my nose, and eventually, she gave in. "I also wanted to give you something."

I extended my hand, and she took my offering with an eyebrow raise. "What's this?"

"It's what I should have given you at your birthday dinner."

"You didn't have to—"

"I know."

"You already baked me a Florida-shaped cupcake . . ."

"That was a tornado," I muttered. "I swear I told you that."

A smile crept to her lips as she tore into the wrapping paper, revealing a floating glass frame with a little speck inside.

"Pretty," she gawked. "What's this yellow thing in the middle?"

"A paint chip."

"A *what*?"

"I picked it up from your grass on moving day."

Casey rolled her head toward me. "You framed a piece of my house?"

"Your old house." I swallowed the lump in my throat. "So you could always remember where you came from . . . and how far you've come."

Silence joined us on the hood, determined to hold out until one of us cried. Not surprisingly, I cracked first.

"Sorry falls kind of short, so I'll ramble until you stop me . . ."

"Sounds like a plan," she replied.

"I haven't been a good friend to you for a while now, Casey, and recently, I haven't been one at all. I just—I just need you to know that this person I've become is temporary. I plan to kill her off the first chance I get."

We winced at the same time.

"Too soon?"

"Way too soon," she replied, wiping away a tear.

"What I'm trying to say is that soon, very soon, I hope the girl I used to be and the one you once were find each other again . . . because they really did have something special."

"I guess I've changed a little, too, huh?"

"I think you should if you want to." I shrugged, running my finger over her rose gold bracelet. "But you never have to."

Casey tossed her arm around my shoulder and squeezed me. I did the same. We peered out into the nearly empty parking lot, just two friends, one frame, and a friendship on the mend.

I made myself busy while I waited on the porch, staring up at the flecked orange clouds. The dark gray sky acted as their canvas, and swirls of rich purples danced about. The expanse looked like a Norah Soros original, if one could be so lucky to obtain such a thing.

"What are you doing at my house?" she barked, the doorbell fading in the background.

I said the girl was gifted, not sweet.

"I need you to know something," I replied, stepping backward down the stairs.

She stood underneath the threshold in a paint-covered T-shirt, holding the door in her hand as if ready to slam it.

"Dean's dad is dating someone."

Norah tilted her head. I could tell she didn't know why I was standing on her cobblestone or why I was telling her the news, but the door remained open.

"He's really going through it," I continued, "and he could really use a friend. I figured that could always be me, but it could always be you . . ."

"*Me*?"

"Why not? You care about him, right?" When I looked beyond the utter detest in her eyes, I could see my answer. "That's what Dean needs: people who care."

Norah's eyes lost focus as if they'd traveled back to another time, a time when Dean was hers. "What? Am I supposed to thank you?"

I stepped away, replying to her question without saying a word, and then, just like that, the ball was in her court.

Maybe it was the burnt-orange Mustang in the driveway or the pile of pebbles I found sitting in the garden, but I was in an old-school kind of mood. I pinched a stone between my fingers and chucked it straight at JC's living room window. Surprisingly, it only took nine of them to work.

A few seconds after he peeked through the blinds, he opened the front door. "You know, they have cell phones for things like this."

I breathed heavily and silently paid homage to every pitcher ever.

"Why are you here?"

"I miss you," I blurted out like I felt pathetic for saying it.

JC glanced left to right, anywhere but at me. "Okay . . . ?"

"You wanna—" I scrunched my nose, still huffing and puffing. "You wanna take a drive?"

Two Led Zeppelin CDs and two hours later, we found ourselves parked down the street from the last place on earth I thought I'd be.

"She worked there?"

"Yeah," I whispered, staring at the two-story glass building. It looked a lot different on Buckets' phone. "She was their waitress."

"I can't believe you guys got into her file."

"Miss it?" I asked, sitting in heavy silence on the other side of the cupholders.

"I'm not sure I've had time to," he replied. "I've only been ghost for like a week."

"And just look at what's unfolded."

"Insane," he mumbled, staring through his windshield in a daze. "At least now you know why she did what she did."

"Yeah . . ."

"You feel better?"

"No," I mumbled. "You?"

"No . . ."

The car fell silent as another one rolled by, its headlights shining straight through Butterfly Café.

"She wanted to be one of us." JC laughed at the thought. "A pretty, perfect, trust fund kid."

"Guess so."

"I wonder if people know how poor it can feel to be rich." He slowly shook his head. "I haven't seen my dad in over a week."

"I haven't really talked to mine in over a year."

JC leaned back with a sigh. "People take one look at our houses and cars and think we've got it made."

“They don’t see the broken relationships.”

“The lost time . . .”

“. . . the emptiness,” I whispered. “You were right all along—it’s almost undoable.”

“She was better off working at a diner and counting her blessings.”

“Especially considering where she is now.” My eyes filled with tears. “Where *do* you think she is now?”

“I don’t know . . .” JC shrugged. “Where do you think she’d want to be?”

I gave it some thought as I stared ahead at the old historic building, tracing its tall windows with glossy eyes. I almost saw her standing there, waltzing down the sidewalk toward work just hoping she’d make enough money to afford a new outfit.

Somewhere along the way, life found her. How could I fault her for that? How could I hate her for what she did to me, knowing the same thing I once set out to find drove her to do it? She’d merely been searching, like me, for a passion so deep she’d do anything to find it.

Souls like that don’t stay buried . . . they *fly*.

JC nodded, and only then did I realize I’d said that last part aloud. He lifted his milkshake into the air. “Here’s to flying.”

“Yeah,” I whispered, lifting mine.

I wondered what ran across Piper's mind when I texted her and told her where to meet me. Moreover, I wondered why she came.

Her Porsche slowed, and she parked it on the curb just like I'd told her to do. "I can't keep doing this."

"Doing what?" I asked, my hands behind my back.

"Meeting you in strange places in the middle of the night."

"Geraldine's wasn't so strange."

"Yeah, well, Principal Winchester's street is." She hugged herself tight, peering sideways at the mansion. "What are we doing here, Sonny?"

It was time to tell her the truth . . . and time to have a good time.

"Getting even," I replied, a brow to the sky.

Piper's furrowed. "What are you talking about?"

"You shouldn't have done what you did to JC. It was selfish and stupid, and it started the downward spiral of so many things." I paused then flipped the script. "But Winchester shouldn't have asked you to."

Months of poor decisions hung between us; we'd each made enough to fill the street. But at the most unlikely time, in the most unlikely of places, I decided to forgive someone who didn't deserve it—myself.

"Grab a roll," I said, pulling my hands forward. "Kyle just killed the cameras."

Piper stared down at the toilet paper, and what I briefly assumed was her refusal was really just the pause before the fun.

"What happens if we get caught?" she asked, grabbing two with a smile.

"I don't know . . . but I don't plan to find out!"

We took off running at the same time, purging our anger by way of a good, old-fashioned teepeeing. Roll after roll, laugh after laugh, Piper and I finally got our payback. And though I never assumed our justice would look like the sky had vomited white slime, it somehow made perfect sense.

LOOSE ENDS: PART TWO

"If I have to knock one more time, I'm kicking the door down!"

Not the sweetest way to start my day, but after Dad's fourth failed attempt at getting me out of bed, I guess I understood.

"I'm up!" I groaned, begrudgingly turning off the snooze. Sixteen ounces of chocolate shake sat at the bottom of my stomach, and that painful achy feeling a person gets from staying up too late was rearing its ugly head.

"I'm taking off! No more snoozing!"

My eyes rolled toward the window. I was expecting to see some sort of sign it was morning, but rainclouds and gray skies awaited me . . . and I wish that were all.

Have you ever had one of those days that just had you? There's no better way to word it, no way to get around the fact that the day completely owns you from the second your head leaves your pillow. No amount of positive thinking or affirmation playlists do a lick of good, because the universe has already decided that nothing good will happen to you for the next twenty-four hours.

You run out of conditioner. You spill your coffee and burn your bagel. You opt out of an umbrella on your way out the door only to turn around and bust your knee in the middle of your school parking lot from running through the rain.

"You okay?" Quinn shouted, extending a hand. I hadn't seen him since the gala when he stood alongside Sawyer in his efforts to intimidate Kyle, but on that morning, he seemed a little more useful.

With no one else around to help, I grabbed hold and stood to my feet. A throbbing pain in my knee almost sent me right back down to the cement.

Quinn forced my arm over his shoulder to make sure that didn't happen, and before I knew it, we were hobbling toward the double doors. "You just ate pavement!"

"Yeah, I was there, thanks!"

"You're probably bleeding," he hollered through the rain. "You should go see the nurse!"

I stared at the death grip he had on my arm and realized his other hand was cupping my waist. The last person I wanted that type of help from was a Bella View kid, but the office seemed so far away, and I wasn't sure I could make it there without him.

Add that to the list under burnt bagel.

"Can you walk me there?" I asked.

Quinn turned his head, his soaked brown curls giving mine a run for their money. "Yeah, I got you."

We made our way through the double doors, collecting quite a few stares from our semi-wet classmates. I guess the situation called for that. Two kids bursting into a quiet hallway, both drenched, one bleeding? I'm sure we looked like a scene straight out of a nineties horror movie.

"Oh, man," Quinn mumbled. "Your leg . . ."

I followed his gaze and glanced down at my jeans. The gash on my knee was nothing to laugh at, and what was left of the fabric had all turned brown.

"Let's get you to the nurse." He shook his hair out and reached for me again—only about ten seconds too slow.

Kyle came in behind us and broke up the madness. He looked like someone who could—an umbrella in his right hand and a large cup of what was probably something warm in his left. "What's going on?" he asked, rushing to my side.

"I fell."

He glanced at Quinn then kneeled beside my knee, ditching his drink to get a closer look. "Shit, Sonny."

"Is it really that bad?"

"Bad enough for you to go to the nurse," he replied, peeling back a flap of fabric.

Quinn lifted his shirt to dry his face. An odd concept, being that it was just as wet. "That's where we were heading."

"He, um—" I shamelessly snuck a peek. "He helped me inside."

"I can walk her there," Quinn continued, looking down at Kyle. "I need to pick up a form anyway."

Kyle turned, and though I couldn't see the look on his face, I knew it wasn't kind. "Why are you telling me that?"

"I—"

"You can leave," he interjected. "We're good."

Quinn's thousand-yard stare spoke volumes—almost as if he wasn't aware we disliked him, almost as if he didn't think we should. "Yeah." He nodded, pulling his eyes off Kyle and placing them on me. "Get some ibuprofen in you."

His sneakers squeaked across the tile as he trekked toward his locker—I watched, and I wasn't sure why. "You didn't have to be so mean," I mumbled, planting my eyes on my new aide.

"That kid stood by and watched while Sawyer made his threats. Don't stand up for him." Kyle hoisted me to my feet. "Can you walk?"

"Yeah, I think so."

"You sure? You can jump on my back."

“I don’t want any more eyes on me,” I replied. I almost felt like I needed to apologize for the morning I was having—or rather, the morning that was having me.

With a little help, I managed to make my way. The hall was quiet—it was still early—but something seemed off. I tried convincing myself that my string of bad luck was due to subconscious nerves. It was the big day after all—Tuesday, to be exact—and our plan was in full effect. We were hours away from Mr. Hill phoning the police, and I wasn’t too naive to realize that fact alone could’ve explained my morning.

Could’ve, but I still wasn’t sure.

“Does this day feel weird to you?” I asked, glancing at Kyle’s scruffy cheek. I feared I knew why he looked so sleepy. Our conversation on the track probably robbed him of a few hours the night before.

“What do you mean?”

“I don’t know . . . something just doesn’t feel right.”

“You’re just having a bad day,” he reassured me. “Everything’s fine.”

I devoured his words, but they did little to sway me. Something was looming overhead, and it wasn’t just the rain clouds.

Kyle opened the office door and bid me farewell. “I have to talk to Singleton before class starts. Think you’ll be okay from here?”

I nodded, though truthfully, I wasn’t sure.

“I have a hoodie in my locker,” he added. “It’s a little wrinkled, but it’s dry. See you in second period.”

“God willing . . .”

Kyle tapped me on my arm then exited through the doorway, leaving me there with my doubts and Ms. Pamela.

“Back again?” she asked, greeting me with a smile that dropped two seconds after seeing my face. “Oh, dear.”

“I got caught in the rain,” I explained. “Is Nurse Tara in?”

“She’ll be here any minute. Would you like to wait for her?”

I squeezed my eyes shut, fearing I needed to drive myself to the nearest medical facility instead. Something told me I needed stitches, but I decided to get another opinion. “Yes, I’ll wait.”

Ms. Pamela helped me to her office then disappeared behind a cracked door. No amount of hard caramel from her candy bowl could’ve made up for the amount of blood I lost waiting, but what I gained from sitting there in the minutes following did. A right place, right time type of conversation, and I just had to share it with someone before I bled out.

“Cliff!”

I considered what was running through Piper’s mind when she saw me with raccoon eyes and a battle wound only hours after I left her or what Norah must’ve thought when I passed by her locker and reached into Kyle’s with scraped-up hands.

Everything seemed so normal the night before—so peaceful—that it was hard to believe how much had changed.

I tugged Kyle's hoodie over my head then dragged myself toward Cliff who met me halfway, his eyebrows scrunched together. "You look like karma just fucked you."

"We need to talk," I replied, falling against the row of lockers with a groan. "Something's going on."

"What happened to your knee?"

"Look, we're not worrying about me, okay?" None the calmer, I glanced over both shoulders before continuing. "I just overheard a conversation between Ron Harrison and Principal Clemmons. They were trying to decide whether they should 'yank them from class.'"

"Yank who from class?"

"They didn't say. They have news—I'm not sure what—but they found something out this morning. I—I couldn't understand everything they were saying, but I heard Ron mention that students will be shocked."

Cliff's eyes started darting around erratically, his gaze unfocused.

"You don't think they found her, *do you*?"

"There's no way," he replied, but his eyes whispered a different story.

To make matters worse, I told him mine. "Something's off, Cliff. This day—my morning—it's like everything that could've gone wrong has."

"What are you talking about?"

"I just—I just feel like something bad is about to happen. Something worse than slicing my knee open."

"You're just paranoid."

"*Paranoid*? How do you explain what Ron Harrison just said?"

"He could've been talking about anything," Cliff replied.

"And what if he was talking about—"

"He wasn't."

"How do you know?"

"Listen to me," he gritted, leaning in closer. "Hill's making the call in a couple of hours, and until we're sure everything worked, we shouldn't be seen speaking to each other. I need you to keep your shit together while we wait."

"I'm trying!"

"Yeah, well, try a little harder." Cliff peered at my leg. "And clean yourself up. You look guilty of something."

Just then, the bell rang, and it sent students scattering. Cliff headed toward first, but I stayed behind, taking a moment to breathe. Unfortunately for me, that moment never came.

"You need some help?"

I opened my eyes to Alice standing taut in a tucked-in, camel-colored shirt and matching wide leg trousers. A period of self-loathing followed, because I knew what I looked like.

"No, thanks," I answered, scooting toward first.

"You do know your knee is sliced open, right?"

"Oh my God, really?"

"I get it," she said, following closely behind. "You're mad about Jacob."

"I'm not."

"It's why you brought up the pact."

"Just calling it like I see it," I replied.

Alice was gaining on me, which wasn't saying much. I wasn't exactly moving very fast. "We made that agreement years ago, Sonny. It was a silly promise between two girls. So much has changed since then."

"Yeah, I can tell."

"That isn't fair," she retorted. "You don't know me. You know nothing about what's happened in my life since we last spoke."

"Then why do you care what I think?" I asked, whipping around once I'd reached my classroom door. I was determined to end one conversation on top that day.

"I don't know!" She shrugged. "I guess I thought we were friends."

"*Friends*? Why, because we shared a bag of sour gummy worms at some stupid football camp?"

Alice crossed her arms. "You don't have to be rude, alright? If you had a problem with me and Jacob, you should have told me when I asked you."

"You and Jacob?" I huffed, staring at her like she was a few fries short. "There is no 'you and Jacob,' Alice. He doesn't even like you."

She slowly unfolded her arms. "Why do you say that?"

"Because he's trying to make me jealous," I fired back. "God, are you seriously too dense to see that?"

Alice's eyes softened just enough to make me realize what I'd done. For a second, I saw the type of girl she used to be before the Crescent changed her: naive. She lowered her chin, tucked her hair behind her ears, then walked swiftly through the crowd and far away from me.

If coming out on top felt like that, maybe being an underdog wasn't so bad after all. I closed my eyes and kicked myself, collecting a few more stares en route to my seat.

As soon as I hit the chair, I dug into my backpack for the gauze I snagged from the nurse's office. With shaking fingers, I unraveled the white cloth and used my car key to cut it. It stuck to my knee and soaked in the blood, immediately needing backup.

I cut more, and after securing it in place, I leaned back in my seat with a sigh. The deep breaths I never got to take I finally took, and I swiped beneath my eyes with the cuffs of Kyle's hoodie.

"Everything's fine," I whispered, reciting the words Kyle had told me. "You're just paranoid," I added, reciting Cliff's, but neither did a thing to help.

Two minutes later, class began, and it was the first time all morning I felt relief, a sense of normalcy. I felt like I was finally crawling out of my thoughts and back to what was.

Of course, *what was* just happened to be worse.

A knock on the door lifted my head. In walked Mr. Harrison and Principal Clemmons, and their chests were puffed like they had something to say. After exchanging a few words with our teacher, they stood before us and relayed the big news.

Ron apologized for the interruption. He apologized for all of them. "You kids have been through a lot," he said. "You've missed a lot of class lately, so we wanted to come to you."

If I still had a heart, I was sure it was pounding. I was sure my face spoke volumes about where my mind was going.

"We received an anonymous tip." He took a breath. "Evidence," he added. "And I'm positive we've found the right person."

My cell phone buzzed, and I reached into my pocket to retrieve it while Principal Clemmons carried on about available resources.

He's going to fucking trade.

Who? I texted Cliff back, slowly stretching my thumb across the screen as I typed discretely. *What*?

Everything was moving so quickly. Everything I feared was coming to me that morning had finally arrived.

"With that being said, I think you all should know that the Westcott Police Department arrested Preston Hill early this morning on arson-related charges."

In the end, we're all just running around tying knots—little tangles that are nothing more than a false sense of security. Because no matter how hard you pull or how well you plan, *there will always be a chance they can come undone*.

ACKNOWLEDGMENTS

My family

My cast

My editor

—

Thank you!

ABOUT THE AUTHOR

Sarah Mello is the self-published author of the Westcott High series. After high school, she pursued her creative nature, which led her into the event industry. She opened a North Carolina wedding venue, which she managed for seven years. However, she never forgot the words of her twelfth-grade English teacher: "You're a writer." She published her first book, Westcott High, in July 2019.

Sarah was born in New York and spent her first five years on Long Island. When she was five, her family moved to Charlotte, NC, where she calls home.

"After writing Chapter Three of Westcott High, I remember thinking how real it felt—as if I were watching my favorite TV show." Sarah goes on to explain the project behind the book. "Bringing my book to life in the way that I did felt like a new concept. I had never seen another author do anything like that, and it was scary at times. But I think there's something to be said about pushing yourself to try new things." Sarah even tackled her own book marketing. "I hope I've shown that you don't necessarily need an abundance of resources to pursue a dream. Just imagine your characters, grab some models and a guy with a camera, and establish a presence on social media."